Baby, It's Cold Outside

STAINED GLASS
PUBLISHING

Chandra Trulove Fry—Cocoa and Mittens
Kasandra Sheckles—Saving Vera
Rubi Rose—Winter Love
Paige Clendenin—Frost Smitten
Deryn Pittar—Thunder Makes Me Cry
Cynthia Staton—I'll Never Let You Fall
La'Keah Shannelle—You Make Me Wanna
Sonya McKinzie—George's Christmas Eve

Cocoa and Mittens
Chandra Trulove Fry

Summary

Cassidy was not looking forward to working on such a cold, snowy day but she had no choice due to a no-show at work. It was already a bad day, but only worsened when she got knocked down in the snow by a little boy. When the boy's father helps her up, she is smitten and can't get the man out of her mind.

Liam could not get the woman out of his mind and instantly regretted scolding his son in front of her. He doubted he would ever see her again. That is, until he got a call to a fire and wound up saving her life. Will things heat up between them or will they go their separate ways?

Biography

Hello! My name is Chandra Trulove Fry. I am a bibliophile, book-dragon. I am married to an amazing tech wizard, and mother to three amazing minions. I am a multi-genre author with several books and stories available now and more to come.

Check out what I have so far and be sure to follow me!

Chandra's Moonlighters:
https://www.facebook.com/groups/288699411565172/

Chandra's Author Page:
https://www.facebook.com/ChandrasAuthorPage/

Chandra's Twitter:
https://twitter.com/ChandraFry12

Chandra's Bookbub:
https://www.bookbub.com/profile/chandra-trulove-fry

Chandra's Amazon Page:

http://www.amazon.com/author/chandratrulovefry/

Website:
https://chandratrulovefry.wixsite.com/themoonlightmuse

Newsletter:
https://weebly.us15.list-manage.com/subscribe?u=10aa6b15a713552d82377c398&id=44579cff5d

Cocoa and Mittens
Chandra Trulove Fry

The bitter wind hit Cassidy as she fought to get to work. She had been called in to cover another coworker who had not made it due to the heavy snowfall. Cassidy didn't understand why the store didn't just close for the day, but the owners were all about making the money. She trudged through the heavy snow, grateful she had worn her waterproof boots instead of the warm fluffy ones. At least in these, her feet stayed dry. The wind seemed to pick up speed and it felt like it was going to rip her jacket right off of her. She held onto it tightly, doing her best to keep it snug against her. All this was just from the parking lot to the front door of the small convenience store she worked at.

She finally made it to the door and just as she was about to open it, the darn thing flew open and something ran into her, knocking her to the ground. Her rear end hit the wet ground with a thud. So much for having more cushion for the pushing. Her tailbone hurt. She looked up to find a young boy about six standing up quickly and brushing himself off. He looked at her with wide eyes full of fright,

"I am so sorry, miss." His eyes welled up with tears.

"Danny! I told you to wait. It's not safe to go out there without me." A man came running out, his voice tinny with trepidation. Danny ran over to the man and fell into his now open arms. "What is it, son? Are you okay? Are you hurt? What happened? Why are you crying?"

His deep voice was gentle, yet frantic. The little boy could not speak, but managed to point his tiny finger in her direction. Cassidy realized then that she was still sitting on the cold ground, completely engrossed in the scene before her. She tried to get up, only to fall and slip again. Her cheeks grew hot and she prayed he would not come her way. No such luck.

"Hey, are you okay?" he asked.

"I can't seem to get up." Images of that commercial with the lady saying she'd fallen but couldn't get up ran through her head, causing her to have a fit of giggles. The man looked at her oddly. "I'm sorry, can you help me up, please?"

"Oh! Of course." He reached down and helped her up with ease. He was a tall man of medium build with sandy blonde hair and brown eyes that sparkled with mirth. His touch made her body tingle all over, causing her to be completely flabbergasted. "What happened?" he asked, curiosity evident.

"I was about to enter the store when your son here came barreling out. We collided and before you know it, I'm sitting on the ground." She laughed. He turned to his boy with a stern look.

"Danny? Did you apologize?"

"He did! Immediately after it happened." Cassidy came to his defense. The man glanced her way, then back to Danny, "See, son, this is why you should listen to me when I tell you stuff. It's so things like this don't happen."

Cassidy had mixed feelings about the way he scolded his son, but felt it best not to interfere. She had a bad habit of meddling in other people's business, so it was very difficult to hold her tongue this time. The wind picked up again, reminding her that this was not good weather to just be standing around in, as well as and reminding her that she was late for work.

"Oh gosh! I need to get inside. I'm so sorry. Thank you...um...what's your name?" she asked.

"I'm Liam. Think nothing of it. We'll be on our way now. Have a good day, miss." He turned away quickly, picked up his son, and headed to his truck before she had a chance to say anything else. She felt a sense of loneliness, causing her to be sad. She didn't want them to go. It felt good to be near them.

Shaking her head, she managed to get inside without further incident. She would need to make herself busy all day just to get thoughts of Liam and Danny out of her head. It would do her no good to constantly think about them when she would most likely never see them again.

It was no use. Her encounter with that handsome guy and his son had her head in the clouds, dreaming of a life with a family, which only caused her day at work to be a mess. By lunchtime, she was a complete wreck. She sat in the break room quietly, eating her lunch, and not quite knowing how to get out of the funk she had placed herself in.

"Cassidy, girl! Where is your head at today?" Monica chastised. If it were anyone else, Cassidy would have chewed her out, but Monica was a good friend and she knew she only had the best of intentions for her.

"I'm sorry. I just had the most bizarre encounter right before work and I can't get it out of my head," Cassidy explained.

"Oooh, do tell. You know I like me some juicy gossip." Monica tapped her long manicured nails on the table.

"Well, first I got knocked down into the snow by a little boy just as I was about to enter the store. Then his dad, I assume, came rushing out, scolding the boy for misbehaving. He was hot to trot. Man, I just can't get him out of my head." Cassidy almost drooled.

"Girl! Cupid got his days mixed up. This is winter, not spring." Monica laughed.

"Right? Help me! I don't know how to get him off of my mind," Cassidy begged.

"All right. Potato," Monica replied, leaving Cassidy confused.

"Potato? What?" Cassidy shook her head, "I'm not following."

"Anytime you get to thinking of this man, say 'potato.' That will get your head cleared and you can focus on your job. Last thing you need is the boss man getting all up in your grill. Not much gets to me, but uh-uh, no way, that man gives me the creeps." Monica lowered her voice to a whisper as she continued, "Besides, honey, I know you need this job."

"Yeah, you're right. I really do." Cassidy agreed, "Okay then, potato."

"Potato." Monica smiled.

Cassidy laughed at the absurdity of it all but had a feeling it was actually going to work.

Monica got up and headed back to work, leaving Cassidy to finish her meal alone. When her break ended, she headed back out to do her job. The rest of her shift had her saying "potato" many times, but it did help her to focus on her tasks and keep up with her work. She was very thankful for having a good friend like Monica. Lucky for her, the boss man did not seem to notice her mishaps at the beginning of her shift.

She was about to lock up after everyone else had left for the day when she was bombarded with the smell of smoke. "What the heck is that?" She followed the smell to the back on into the bakery section of the store. The entire area was covered in smoke and flames, causing Cassidy to cough and sputter. She covered her nose and mouth with her sweater while grabbing her phone to dial 911. She attempted to make her way back to the front when a beam fell in front of her path. Cassidy freaked out and ran toward another aisle, but could not see due to the smoke.

Her phone rang a few times before someone responded, "911, what's your emergency?"

"The store is on fire!" Cassidy managed to choke out. Her voice was raspy and it was getting harder to breathe.

"Which store, ma'am? Ma'am?" the lady asked. It was getting difficult for Cassidy to concentrate and she barely registered the lady on the line.

"Huh? What? Oh...it's, uh...Mencer's Mercantile." She coughed as she fell to the floor.

"Ma'am, are you safe? We have first responders on their way. Ma'am? Ma'am?" The lady continued to try and get Cassidy's attention, but it was no use. Cassidy had passed out from the fumes.

Liam had just tucked his son in when he got the call. Thankfully, his roommate, Justice, was able to stay with Danny while he booked it to the fire station. Minutes later, they were on their way to the very store he'd been in earlier that day. What were the odds? He'd left that store with nothing but that beautiful woman on his mind. He had kicked himself for having treated her so rudely. She was only trying to be helpful, but in his panicked state, he had merely brushed her aside like she was nothing. He wished he had played things out more smoothly. He ran scenarios over and over in his head, about how he treated her like a princess and got her number. Then his thoughts went into a more intimate direction in which he needed to take a cold shower. It had just been too long.

Now he was heading to that store due to a huge fire that seemed to be out of control. They arrived to find the store in a blaze. Liam didn't think that the building was going to make it. They should just let it burn down.

"Sir, they believe that the call was made from inside and the woman who called may still be in there, unconscious. Do we dare go in?" one of his team asked. Liam took a good look at the building and assessed the fire.

"It would be risky, but I'm willing to go in." He responded.

"Roger that. We'll keep working on it from here." The man went back and relayed the news. Liam rolled his shoulders up and prepared to hopefully save a life. He took off instinctively, not allowing himself to change his mind. He rammed the front door open and was instantly met with thick smoke. He was grateful for the mask and breather. He treads through debris and smoke in search for the woman who had called. Looking about, he searched aisle after aisle. Nearing the far end of an aisle, he spotted her passed out on the floor. He ran up to her, checked her vitals quickly. She was hanging in there. He pulled his mask off and put it over her head, then picked her up and hefted her over his shoulder while he maneuvered out of the charring remains of the store.

A beam fell just behind him, causing him to pick up his pace toward the front of the store. He was never one to panic, but he was cutting things close with this fire. He was much relieved when he made it to the front and pushed his way through the door. Something exploded, causing him to pitch forward and almost lose his footing. He managed to right himself without dropping the poor woman. The inferno behind him was getting much hotter. The paramedics ran up to him with a gurney and helped him place her on it. He watched as they took off the mask and handed it to him. To his surprise, the woman on the gurney was the same woman he had met earlier that day. He continued to watch as they placed an oxygen mask on her and wheeled her to the ambulance.

"Good job, Liam!" His friend Mitchell slapped him on the back.

"All in a day's work, man." Liam answered back as they both headed to the truck to help continue putting out the fire.

"I think it's useless at this point," Mitchell said.

"I agree. Let's safeguard the perimeter and let it burn down," Liam commanded. They did as he said, securing the area to make sure the fire would not spread anywhere else. Liam watched the fire closely as he continued to delegate the tasks that needed to be done. All the while, in the back of his mind, thoughts of the condition of that woman tormented him.

———————//———————

Cassidy's eyes felt heavy as she tried to open them. She could hear sounds of machines bleeping, and it felt like she things were attached to her. When she finally opened her eyes, she was able to see that she was in a hospital room. An IV was attached to her arm, and she was hooked up to a machine keeping track of all of her vitals. A nurse came in to check on her and noticed she was awake.

"Oh, good! I'm so glad you are awake. I'll alert the doctor right away." She was a young nurse, and her cheery demeanor made Cassidy want to smile.

"What happened?" Cassidy coughed.

The nurse came over with a cup of ice and said, "Don't you worry about that just now. Let's focus on getting you better first. Here, eat some ice chips. That will help with the dry mouth."

Cassidy took the cup and started to eat a couple of ice chips as she was told to. The nurse adjusted her bed so Cassidy could sit up more.

"How's that, hun?"

"Much better. Thank you," Cassidy said with a much clearer voice.

"I'll go alert the doctor. He should be with you soon," the nurse said kindly as she left the room.

Cassidy looked around the room still in a bit of a haze and confused as to why she was there. Her mind was foggy and it hurt every time she tried to recall what happened. Exhausted from the efforts she drifted off to sleep.

"Miss Matthews! I'm happy to hear you are alert." The sound of an unknown masculine voice startled her awake.

"Goodness, you scared me," she cried out when she realized it was the doctor.

"I'm so sorry, dear. I thought that you were still awake. I didn't mean to frighten you. I'm Dr. Linzet." He held out his hand for her to shake. Cassidy took the hand and shook it lightly as he sat down next to her. "I understand you have no memory of what happened?"

"No, I'm afraid I don't. I keep trying to recall things, but it hurts my head to do so. Can you please tell me what happened?" Cassidy pleaded.

"You were trapped by a fire in the market you work at. Luckily for you, one of the firemen braved entering the building and saved your life. I'm sorry to have to tell you this, but your workplace burnt completely to the ground," he informed her.

"Did anyone get hurt?" Cassidy worried that one of her co-workers may not have made it.

"No one did. It would seem you were the last one there," he stated simply, no accusation in his voice.

"I don't remember a fire. I don't even remember what happened on that day. I am so confused." Cassidy started to panic.

The doctor placed his hand gently on hers and said, "Now, dear, it's all right. Short-term memory loss is common. I am most certain you will remember everything real soon." He was an elderly doctor, and definitely had good bedside manners. His words helped soothe her and she was able to calm down.

"I would like to thank the firefighter who saved me. Is that possible?" she inquired.

"Actually, I'm glad you said something. That very person wants to visit with you as soon as you are ready for visits. Would you like me to inform him he can come to see you?" He smiled.

"Yes, please. That would be nice." She wondered why he would want to see her. Maybe he just wanted to make sure she was really okay. That made sense. Dr. Linzet asked her many questions as he did a thorough exam on her.

"You seem to be recovering nicely. I don't think you'll be here for more than a few days. In the meantime, I recommend you take this time to rest and allow your body to heal." He smiled again as he left the room.

Cassidy closed her eyes as she tried to recall yet again, what happened the day before. She stopped right away as the headaches started again. Trying to get her mind off of things, she ate a few more ice chips and turned on the TV, browsing through it to find something that might be of interest. She finally stopped on some game show and was able to get lost in it.

An hour later, the nurse came in, asking if she'd like some dinner. Starving, she heartily placed an order and her food arrived shortly after. It wasn't the greatest, but at least it was edible. A burger was still a burger. She lay back with a full belly and went back to watch random stuff on the TV.

A knock on the door, causing her to jump. She turned to the door just as a tall, handsome man entered. He seemed very familiar to her.

"Hi, I was told I could visit you now. Is now a good time?" he asked kindly.

"Oh, yeah. Sure." Cassidy fumbled for words. He walked over and sat in a chair near her bed.

"How are you doing?" The concern in his voice was evident. He seemed genuinely worried about her and that made her feel special.

"Physically, I'm doing really well. The only issue I seem to be having is some temporary short-term memory loss. I honestly cannot remember anything about yesterday," Cassidy explained.

"I'm glad you are doing well. I'm sure that the memories will come back soon. Oh, I brought you some cocoa. I wasn't sure if it was okay to do so, and then I thought right before I entered, 'what if she doesn't like cocoa?' It won't hurt my feelings a bit if you don't." He laughed. She liked the sound of his deep baritone laugh. It felt like entering a safe harbor.

"I absolutely love cocoa! Thank you." She exclaimed as she reached out for the cup that she hadn't even noticed he had been holding the whole time. She'd been too focused on his chiseled features more than anything else. "What is your name?"

"Oh, I'm such a dolt. My name is Liam. A pleasure to meet you, Cassidy." He did a slight bow of the head, reminding her of a Jedi.

"How do you know my name?" She giggled.

"Oh, I kind of looked you up so I was able to find you here. I hope that's okay. I wasn't trying to be a creeper or all stalkerish. I mostly wanted to make sure you were alright and to apologize." He lowered his head, eyes downcast.

"Apologize? For saving my life? I'm so glad you did!" Cassidy's mind was boggled. What did this man have to apologize for?

"Ah, you don't remember any of what happened yesterday?" he asked.

"No. Sorry." His question made her feel like she had missed something very important. Something even more important than being trapped in a fire.

"We had an encounter earlier that day. My son ran out the door, not listening to me. I came out to find he had knocked you on your rear into the snow. I felt horrible, but my embarrassment kept me from really helping you. I wanted to say that I'm sorry for being a grade-A jerk to you and for overreacting in the chastisement of my son. He's a good kid, just a little hyper." Liam had a wistful look as he talked about his son.

"He really knocked me over? That's funny." Cassidy chuckled.

"Well, I'm just glad no harm was done. I do have another confession to make, though." His cheeks grew red.

"Oh?" Cassidy grew curious. What else did this man want or do?

"Ever since that encounter I have not been able to get you out of my head. You are a beautiful woman, Cassidy, and I would very much like to get to know you." He coughed to hide his embarrassment.

"Wow, I don't know what to say." Cassidy blinked, wondering if this was all just a bizarre dream.

"Say you'll go to dinner with me," he asked boldly. He figured he'd already gotten this far, why not keep going?

"I'm kind of stuck in this hospital for the next few days." She smirked.

"After you get out, you goose." The twinkle of victory shone in his eyes, bringing a blush to Cassidy's face.

"I would love to," she replied, suddenly shy. Liam took her hand in his and looked her in the eyes,

"Since you'll be here for the next few days, do you mind if I continue to visit so we can get to know one another?" The warmth of his touch spread through her body like wildfire, causing her mind to wander as the images of things to come popped into her head.

"I'd like that," she whispered. Words became evasive as she tried to think of what else to say when Liam's cell rang. He took a quick look at who was calling and frowned.

"I'm sorry. Do you mind if I take this call?"

"Of course not. Go for it." She shooed him.

He hit the green button, "Hello? Yes, this is he." He paused, "He forgot his mittens? Really? Yes, I can bring them to him. Boys. They think they are superheroes."

Cassidy could not hide her smirk and she could hear the teacher on the phone laughing. Liam hung up and looked at Cassidy with sad eyes. "I truly hate having to go. It would seem Danny forgot to bring his mittens to school today and he needs them so he can participate in building a snowman. I'll come by again tomorrow." He leaned down and kissed her lightly on the forehead, then left the room quickly.

When Liam said Danny's name, it opened the floodgates of Cassidy's mind. She suddenly recalled everything that had happened that day. Her face grew flushed as she relived every moment like it was happening just then. It was almost too much to bear and must have been bigger than she'd thought as the nurses came running in to check on her. They gave her a sedative to help calm her down so she could rest. She was grateful the meds worked quickly as she drifted off into a drug-induced sleep.

Cassidy woke to a bright morning as the rays of the sunrise entered her room. It was a stunning view that she enjoyed once she was able to adjust her eyes to see it. The events of the evening and the day before started to bombard her mind again, only this time, less severely. She was shocked things had turned out the way they had. As she thought about Liam and the things that transpired between them, her face flushed and body grew warm. He had called her beautiful and wanted to get to know her. He wanted to go on a date with her.

At first, she was ecstatic, but then she remembered he had a son. That made things very different in her book. Where was Danny's mother? Liam wouldn't ask her out if he were married would he? What did this mean for the future? More questions began to consume her as she considered every option possible. She finally decided she would just be up front with him and ask him all the necessary questions. To her, it was important that they start out by being completely honest with one another.

A knock on the door brought her out of her thoughts. She turned to the door eagerly, hoping to see Liam's handsome face.

A woman walked in quietly and asked, "Cassidy, honey, you here?"

"Monica! Yes. Get your butt in here!" Cassidy greeted excitedly. Monica shut the door behind her then came around to where Cassidy was sitting up in her bed.

"Girl! How the heck are you?" Monica asked as she gave Cassidy a light hug.

"I'm doing okay. It's been a wild couple of days." Cassidy sighed.

"I was worried sick about you. No one would say a thing for a while, then suddenly I get a random call telling me that you are in the hospital, but recovering. I just wanted to hit them." Monica growled.

"It's okay. I worried about you too, actually. I wasn't sure if anyone else got caught up in that scariness. Did they ever find out what happened?" Cassidy asked.

"Oh, hold up. You won't believe this." Monica held up a perfectly manicured finger. "Our old boss man, well he had this great idea that he was going to set his place on fire and collect the insurance. He planned it to be an accident and all that. I guess he wasn't thinking about other people's lives, though, was he?"

"I can't believe it. What a scoundrel." Cassidy grimaced, "How did they find out?"

"Well, I don't know if there was a bit of decency somewhere in there, or if he thought you might sue the pants off of him, which you totally should, but he went and confessed the whole thing! Can you believe that?" Monica snapped her fingers.

"That's nuts!" Cassidy agreed.

"So, anything good happen here?" Monica had a knowing look.

"Actually, yes." Cassidy smiled coyly.

"Oh?" Monica raised her well-sculpted brow.

"You know that firefighter who saved me?" Cassidy led on.

"What about him?" Monica tapped the rail of Cassidy's bed, clearly growing impatient.

"Potato." Cassidy winked.

"Potato?" Monica questioned.

"Yes, potato." Cassidy wiggled her brows. Monica's eyes grew huge as her mouth dropped open. She sat back in the chair with animated hands.

"No! No no no no no! You saying?" She put her hand to her mouth. "Are you saying what I think you're saying?"

"Yes!" Cassidy burst out in laughter, "I am saying 'potato'!"

Monica leaned her elbows on the rail and placed her chin on her hands, "Girl, you have got to tell me everything. And by everything, I mean *everything*!"

Cassidy giggled at her best friend's excitement. She was more than ready to share every last juicy bit of gossip about Liam with her. It was the beginning of something new and exciting, and she was eager to let her friend in on that excitement.

Saving Vera
Kasandra Sheckles

Summary

When Vera's husband died in an accident two years before in a winter time accident, she fell into a deep depression leaving her young daughter to care for herself most of the time. Two years after the untimely death, Vera gets word that her foster parents have died and she must return home for the funerals and to take care of their last wishes. While there, she meets the handsome caretaker her parents had hired to help them maintain their property in the later years.

Mac took to Vera right away but he could tell that she had been hurt and her guard was up. He knew she deserved love and happiness but he wasn't sure she was ready to let it in. When Vera finds out her husband faked his death and had another family, he hoped she would give him the chance to show her what love really could be.

Will Vera overcome her depression? Will winter become her favorite season again? Will she let her guard down and let Mac in? Find out in Saving Vera!

Biography

Kasandra Sheckles is the author of *His Love for Lexi* and has a short story in the *Time Stoppers* Anthology, with more coming out this year. Kasandra lives in Southern Illinois with her husband, Chris, and stepsons, as well as four dogs.

Saving Vera
Kasandra Sheckles

Vera

"Mom!" I heard my daughter yell from down the hall. I knew I needed to see what she wanted, but I was barely able to keep myself awake. I had been this way for almost a year, just doing the bare minimum for my child. I felt guilty, but couldn't make myself stay motivated. I knew I was a disappointment, possibly even an embarrassment to my daughter, but the depression made me not want to work to fix it.

It was winter. I hated winter. At one time, winter was my favorite season, but two years ago, that changed. Winter took my love from me. The only love I'd ever known. My husband, Marco, had been the only person to ever really love me unconditionally. I was born to teenage parents who didn't want to accept the consequences for their actions, so they abandoned me in the hospital. I spent my childhood in and out of foster homes, being abused in one way or another.

When I was sixteen, I was placed with an older couple whose only son had been killed in a military training accident. They showed me love, but I had to maintain a certain grade point average, and I was the only one to clean the house and cook meals. I didn't mind though, at least I wasn't getting beat on every day. When I graduated from high school, and technically aged out of the foster care system, they allowed me to stay with them and attend college. Once I was finished at the two-year college, I transferred out of state to finish my degree in business management. That was where I met Marco.

I spotted him my first day, but was too shy to talk to him. We had been there a month before either one of us had the nerve to speak to the other. We were inseparable during our time there, and after we both graduated, he proposed, and we married six months later. We enjoyed ten years together, and our wonderful daughter, Mia, made our lives so much better. Mia was about to be ten, and was a better parent than me most days. We both took it really hard when Marco passed away, but she seemed to climb out of her darkness and I had not.

When I didn't respond to her yell, Mia opened my bedroom door and tiptoed inside. I pretended to be asleep, so she wouldn't know I was just being lazy and didn't want to get out of bed. She leaned down and kissed my cheek and left my room. A few minutes later, I heard the front door shut as she headed for the bus stop. I let my guilt consume me and I cried until I exhausted myself and went to sleep.

I woke to the sound of someone pounding on my door. I sighed as I got up and threw my robe on. I made my way to open the door, where I find an older man in a suit.

"Hello, miss. Are you Vera Thomas? Formerly Vera Marshall?"

I nodded and stepped aside so the man could come in. I motioned for him to sit and I sat across from him, wondering what was going on.

"Mrs. Thomas, I am Brad Jenkins. I am the attorney for Mike and Bev Collins. They were your foster parents for a few years, correct?"

I nodded again and went to the fireplace. I grabbed their picture off the mantel. I handed it to Brad and he looked at it carefully.

"I am here today because they have passed away. They were in a car accident two days ago. They requested you be at the service and the reading of their will."

I looked at him in shock. The only people that had ever treated me decent were gone. The only family I had now was Mia, and I was destroying her with my behavior. I knew going home was probably what I needed, but it was winter. I never left the house in the winter unless it was necessary.

"I'm sorry, Mr. Jenkins. I can't go to the service. I don't leave in the winter. I can't leave in winter."

Brad looked like he wanted to push the issue, but stopped himself. Just as he was about to say something, Mia walked in the door.

"Mom! You're out of bed! This is great!"

Brad looked at me, horrified, as I hugged Mia and kissed her on the cheek.

"I've been sick, so I haven't been out of bed much. I am feeling better, though." I hoped he bought it as I introduced him to Mia and explained why he was there.

"I am sorry about grandma and grandpa, Mom. I really think we should go and say goodbye to them."

I knew my girl was right, but I didn't want to tell her I was terrified to leave the safety of our home because I didn't want to end up like her father. I needed to be strong for my baby girl, or at least pretend to be.

Brad left, leaving his number in case I changed my mind. I stared at his card and thought about what I should do. I knew that I needed to go and pay my respects to them, but my fear was too great. I baked a frozen pizza for Mia and me as she did her homework. Once we ate and she got a bath, I told her to watch TV, and I went back to my bed.

I laid in bed and turned Brad's card over and over in my fingers as I thought about what to do. During dinner, Mia had said that we should go. She wanted to say goodbye and thought it would be good for me too. She was so mature for her age, and I knew that was my fault. I decided that the next morning, I would see about getting some counseling so I could be better for my girl. Then I would call Brad and let him know we'd come. I drifted to sleep to the sound of Mia laughing at the TV.

The next morning, I heard Mia's alarm go off and I got up to make sure she had gotten up. She seemed happy that I was up with her as she got dressed. I made us a bowl of scrambled eggs and Mia ate them like it was the first time she'd had eggs. I laughed at her as she gobbled them down.

"Slow down, silly, there's plenty, and you've got lots of time."

She smiled as she finished her eggs and put her bowl in the sink.

"I don't want more eggs, Mom. I just wanted to get done faster so we could have more time together. I like it when you get up with me in the mornings."

My heart lurched in my chest and I wanted to cry. Losing Marco had taken away my desire to live, and me letting that happen was hurting my girl.

Once Mia was on the bus, I called and got my counseling set up, then called Brad to let him know we'd be coming to the service. After I finished the call with him, I showered and began to pack for our trip. By the time I finished packing, it was time for me to go to my first counseling appointment. I was excited about getting myself better.

I walked out of the counselor's office feeling better than I had in a long time. I went home and cooked Mia supper, which is something I hadn't done in a long time. I fried chicken and mashed potatoes. I couldn't wait for her to get home. She was going to be so surprised. I was opening cans of corn when she came through the front door.

"Mom! You're up! This is great! What smells so good?"

I smiled as I walked her into the kitchen and sat her plate on the table. She eagerly grabbed her piece of chicken and began eating. I grabbed my plate and began eating beside her. As we ate, she told me about her day and asked about mine. As we talked, I felt a bit of the normalcy we'd had when Marco was alive had returned. It made me feel good to know I had made my little girl happy. The smile on her face told me she was exactly that.

After supper was finished and the kitchen cleaned, I told her we were taking the trip and we finished packing. I told her we were leaving with Mr. Jenkins early the next morning, so she quickly showered and got ready for bed. I sat with her for a while, watching her favorite cartoon and listened to her giggle. Once she fell asleep on my lap, I carried her to her bed and tucked her in. I closed her door and made my way to the shower. I soaked up the hot water and thought about the twists and turns my life had taken the past few years. I knew I had to take charge of my life and reclaim the happiness that was taken from me by Marco's death. I knew he wouldn't want me to be the way I had been. I also knew the longer I stayed that way, the more damage I was doing to Mia.

The next morning, Mia woke me and we prepared the house for our departure. I had told the school the day before that Mia wouldn't be in class for a few days. Now all that was left to do was notify the post office. I did that with one phone call and we waited for Mr. Jenkins to arrive. As we waited, I made sure we had everything we needed, and everything was turned off. I didn't want to come back to outrageous bills, or a burned down house.

Mr. Jenkins arrived with a smile on his face and put our luggage in the trunk of his car. I was a bit nervous still, even though I wasn't the one driving. I buckled my seat belt and nervously played with the hem of my coat.

Mr. Jenkins reached over and placed his hand on mine, "It's okay, my dear. Try not to worry. You are in capable hands."

I felt bad for making him think I didn't trust him. It wasn't him at all—it was the time of year. The season that took everything from me.

"Mr. Jenkins, I don't want you to think I am afraid of your driving. It's not you. It's the fact that it's winter. That's all."

I watched as Mr. Jenkins' face clouded over, and he nodded in understanding. I wondered if my foster parents had told him about my husband's death. We traveled the rest of the way in silence as Mia slept in the backseat.

I had forgotten how big the place was and was surprised when we pulled into the half circle driveway. I couldn't believe I had lived here, and Mia couldn't either. I watched her as she gazed in awe at the giant house I called home for the last few years of my adolescence. I took Mia by the hand and led her up the steps to the front door. We entered the house and I couldn't believe what I saw. Everything was still the same as it had been when I lived there. They had changed nothing over the years. I was eager to see if my room was still the same as well. I led Mia up the stairs and slowly opened the door to the room that had once been mine.

I was amazed at the memories that came flooding back as I walked around my old room. It was the same as the day I left. They hadn't changed a thing or gotten rid of any of my things. I sat on the bed and began to cry. For the first time since going to live with them, I realized they really had loved me. Yes, they had made me cook and clean, but I understood why they did that. They wanted me to learn to do those things so I could be self-sufficient and a good wife and mother. I noticed that Mia was watching me with a concerned look on her face, so I composed myself and headed back downstairs to get the bags from Mr. Jenkins' car.

When we reached the bottom of the stairs our bags were being brought inside by Mr. Jenkins and another man I didn't recognize.

"Mr. Jenkins, I could have gotten our bags. You didn't have to do that. I appreciate it, though." I eyed the other man warily as he smiled at me. Mr. Jenkins used his hands and made some gestures to the man and he nodded and went outside.

"Call me Brad, please. Being called Mr. Jenkins makes me feel old. As for the young man who was with me, his name is Mac Thompson. Mike hired him about six months ago to help with upkeep around here. It had become a bit too much for Mike, and I think he also took pity on Mac. No one really wants to hire a deaf guy for hard labor jobs, and Mac doesn't belong in an office."

I watched out the window as Brad spoke, and he seemed to be right. Mac didn't look like the office type at all. I instantly became concerned for him and wondered what would happen now that Momma and Daddy were gone.

"What's he going to do now that Mom and Dad are gone? Does he have anywhere else he can go?"

Brad looked at me with a grim look on his face and shook his head. I looked out the window to see Mac kneeling, and Mia in front of him. He was teaching her a sign for something.

I pushed the window up and leaned my head out. I yelled her name and she looked toward the window. I waved her to the window and she ran over to me.

"Mia, you need to come in and leave Mac to his work. He doesn't need you bothering him."

She looked disappointed as she ran over to him, and wrote on a piece of paper. She walked toward the house as he read the paper she handed him. He looked at the window, and his gaze took my breath. I stepped away from the window and took our bags up the stairs and unpacked them. I had to stay focused on the task ahead. I couldn't get distracted by a pretty farm boy.

19

The next morning, I woke with the sun shining in my face, and Mia gone from the room. I dressed in the outfit I'd brought for the service and headed downstairs. I found Mia in the kitchen with Brad and Mac. They were all dressed and ready to go. Mac looked at me and smiled as he put his hand in front of his face and fanned his fingers across his face.

Brad laughed at my confused look and told me it was the sign for beautiful. I grabbed a pen and wrote "thank you" on a piece of paper and he smiled.

We headed to the service and I wondered if I would be able to keep myself together. I tried keeping myself together once we got to the funeral home, but I fell apart. They had meant so much to me and now they were gone. I felt strong arms wrap around me and looked up to see Mac. I leaned into him as he soothed me. I was grateful for this stranger in my time of need.

Mac

I hadn't known Vera personally since I came to work for the Collins family only six months before, but I felt I knew her from things I had been told about her. I watched her as she fell to pieces in front of their caskets and I couldn't resist the urge to comfort her. I was nervous that she might reject me, but she leaned into me and let me console her. I held her as she shook with violent sobs. I knew this woman had endured horrible pain in her life and had felt something special for these people with the way she let it out like that.

I was finally able to calm her, and I helped her to her seat beside her daughter, Mia. I started to walk away to go find a seat in the back, but she grabbed my hand and pulled me into the empty chair on the other side of her. She slipped a note in my hand that read: *you were just as much their family as I was. You can sit here with me.* I was blown away by her kindness and consideration. My life hadn't been a very happy one until I came to know the Collins family and started working for them. Mike was one of the few people in my life to really take a chance on me. Most people hadn't wanted to hire me to do farming or ranch work because I couldn't hear and wouldn't know if an animal was coming after me or if something was going to fall on me. Mike was different he had hired me and trained me to make sure I knew the job and could handle it.

They had told me about their daughter often and the tragedy she had endured. And now here she was, enduring another one. I put my arm around her as she started to shake again, and my heart broke to see her in so much pain. Once the service was over and we went to the cemetery, I sat beside her once again and had to help her walk back to the car. I wondered if she was going to be okay after I left. With her parents gone now, there was no need for me to stay, and she'd most likely be selling the place. It pained my heart to think about leaving. That place had become my home and I felt like I belonged there. We arrived at the church for the after-service potluck dinner and she held on to me during the entire thing. By the time we got back to the house, Brad had to unlock the door, so I could carry her inside. She had fallen asleep against me, the exhaustion evident on her face.

I carried her up the stairs and laid her on her bed while Mia covered her up. I smiled down at the little girl and we went downstairs. I spent a little time with her, teaching her signs and playing card games before heading out to do the evening chores. I was surprised to find that Mia had followed me out and signed to me that she wanted to help me. I smiled and showed her what she needed to do. Before I knew it, we had the chores done.

As we were headed back to the house, snow started to fall.

I watched as Mia twirled around and held her tongue out. I smiled as she ran around the yard and tried to get snow in her mouth. I motioned for her to come inside with me. I knew if I kept her outside too long, her mother wouldn't be happy with me. I knew I had better cherish what time I had left here because Vera would soon be telling me to leave. I pushed the sad thoughts away and enjoyed the time I was spending with Mia. We had just started to cook supper when Vera came down the stairs. She looked a bit more rested than she had earlier, but she still looked exhausted.

I pulled a chair out and motioned for her to sit and she smiled as she sat. She helped Mia and me prepare supper and we ate together as if we were a family. It appeared they weren't talking, so I concentrated on my food. I finished my plate and started the dishes while they finished up. As I turned to grab Mia's plate, I noticed Vera was crying. I sat beside her and put my arm around her and held her until she calmed down. She mouthed "I'm sorry," and I waved my hand and grabbed some paper. I told her it was no problem and Mia helped me finish the kitchen.

After supper, Brad showed up and told us the reading of the will was the next day and we all had to be there. I wondered why I needed to be there, considering I wasn't family. I had only worked with them for six months. I decided I wouldn't fight it, and I'd go in respect of them. I knew in the off chance that they did leave me something, I'd give it to Vera. She would probably benefit from what they gave more than I would. We all sat around the fireplace and Brad and Vera exchanged stories of the Collins family and for the first time in a long time, I wished I had my hearing.

I lost my hearing in an accident involving fireworks when I was twelve. I hadn't really missed it much until now. I wanted so badly to hear what they were saying. I knew what they were saying because I learned to read lips, but I wanted to hear it. I wanted to hear Vera's voice. I was drawn to her like a moth to a flame, and I didn't understand why. We'd only known each other a couple days, but I found myself wishing I could hear her voice and the innocence of her laughter. She hadn't smiled much since being back and I understood why. But I found myself wanting to make her smile.

Once Brad left and everyone else went to bed, I sat in the living room and looked around the place that had been my home for six months and wondered where I would go. My parents had passed away in an accident shortly after I lost my hearing, and my grandma who finished raising me passed away a year before I started working for the Collins. A part of me hoped that they had left me something to remember them by, but another part of me knew that it probably wouldn't happen. Vera was their daughter everything was hers. I felt my eyelids grow heavy, so I turned off the fireplace and headed to my room at the back of the hall. I drifted to sleep, dreaming of what Vera's voice might sound like.

I woke with a start as I dreamed of the accident which took my hearing. It was still dark out, but I couldn't go back to sleep, so I decided to get up and get started on the morning chores. I made my way to the kitchen to find Vera sitting at the table. I motioned toward the coffee pot and she nodded her head. I started the pot and waited for it to finish as I started to cook breakfast. We ate together as Mia still slept and she thanked me for being there for them both. We cleared the table and washed the dishes. My heart pounded as I stood next to her. She made me feel things I hadn't felt in a long time. I knew I shouldn't feel the things I did because I was only going to get hurt in the end, but I couldn't help myself.

My thoughts were interrupted by a splash of water in my face. I turned to look at Vera and I could tell she was laughing, and I wished once again I could hear it. I splashed her back and she took a handful of suds from the sink and rubbed them on my cheek. Her touch ignited something in me that had been dormant for a long time and I swore I saw a sparkle in her eye that hadn't been there before. We cleaned up our mess and I headed out to do the morning chores.

When I came back inside, I found Vera and Mia ready to go to the will reading. I quickly washed up and we headed out.

I felt the tension in the air and I knew Vera was nervous. We arrived at Brad's office and he welcomed us inside. Once everyone was seated, Brad opened the will and began reading. They left everything they had to Vera and her daughter Mia, with the exception that I stay on as hired help and they stay in the home for at least six months before deciding whether to sell or not. Vera looked at me with a sideways glance and gave me a small smile. It was hard for me to read their lips for the tears that filled my eyes. No one had ever treated me like family as they had and I was so grateful. They had also given Vera permission to give me the account information to the trust they'd set up for me as my salary. I was overcome with emotion at the love they showed me when they didn't have to.

After tears were shed and hugs were shared, we left Brad's office and headed to the café on Main Street. Since it was just down the road, a bit from Brad's office, we decided to walk. We were half a block from the café when Vera stopped suddenly, frozen in place. I followed her gaze to see a tall man in a suit with a woman and toddler. I gave Vera a questioning look, but she wasn't paying attention to me. She stared straight at the man with the other woman. Mia stood beside her mother, much the same, frozen in place, staring at the couple and the child. I waved my hand in front of their faces, but they weren't seeing me.

I watched as Vera opened her mouth and the man turned to look at her. His face turned from happy to horrified in an instant. Mia let go of her mother's hand and made her way to the edge of the road. She looked both ways before she took off toward the man. I tried to grab her, but she dodged my hand. I could tell Vera was yelling, and I was frustrated that I couldn't hear what she was saying. She was crying hysterically, which made it difficult for me to read her lips.

Vera crossed the street to retrieve Mia, and as I watched their interaction, I gathered that the man was Marco, her supposedly deceased husband. I couldn't believe any man would do something so heinous as fake their death to a woman like Vera or a sweet kid like Mia. Anger welled up in me and I had to walk away before I did something stupid. I went ahead to the café and ordered a cup of coffee. I drank my coffee and waited for them to show up. When an hour had passed and they haven't shown up, I paid for my coffee and made my way back to the truck. I looked across the street, but they weren't where I had walked away from them. The other people were gone too, and I wondered if they had left together.

I drove back to the house expecting to find it empty, but Brad's car and another car were in the driveway. I hopped out of the truck and ran inside. Brad was at the table with a crying Vera on one side of him and Mia on the other. When Mia saw me, she jumped up and ran to me. I grabbed her up into a hug as she began to cry on my shoulder. I looked at Brad and he signed that he'd explain it to me later. I nodded and comforted Mia as she continued to cry.

The couple from earlier sat on the couch and they looked like they had been found guilty of a crime. Once Mia finally calmed down, I let her down to the floor and I took a chair beside her mother. I tried to grab her hand, but she pulled away from me. I told myself not to be offended, but I couldn't help it. I stood and went to the pole barn and laid in the makeshift bunk that I had made when I started working for the family.

I didn't know what was going to happen now her husband was back from the dead, but I knew it didn't change how I felt about her. I tried to tell myself I still had a shot, but deep down I didn't believe that. No one wants to love the deaf guy.

Vera

I couldn't believe what was happening. My heart felt like it had been ripped from my chest and put through a meat grinder before being thrown back in my chest. Marco was the last person I ever expected to see. I was filled with anger when I saw him and the woman he was with. We had argued in the street and Brad had seen what was happening and suggested we go back to the house and talk. I felt bad for leaving Mac at the café without an explanation and I hoped he'd let me make it up to him.

The other woman hadn't seemed surprised at all. As we talked, Marco revealed to me that he had become involved with a group of really awful people. When he found out how awful they were, he threatened to rat them out to the police. He knew they would kill him if he did that and possibly us too, so he made the decision to fake his death. To me, it didn't matter what the reason was. I felt there was no excuse for it and I refused to hear another word he said.

Brad was at the table comforting Mia and me when Mac burst through the door. The way Mia ran to him for comfort brought tears to my eyes. She had developed such a close bond with him already. It was nice to see him pay attention to her. Marco had always been too busy with work to play with her and now I knew why. I watched Marco as he squirmed uncomfortably, watching Mac give his daughter the attention he never gave her.

Once he had calmed Mia down, I asked everyone except Marco to step outside for a few moments. After everyone went outside, I sat across from him on the other couch. I sat still and waited until I could breathe evenly, and my pulse slowed. I watched him as he pulled at the collar of his shirt and I relished the thought of him nervous and uncomfortable. He had put Mia and me through unbelievable hell for the past two years, and he had run off and started a new life. I sucked in a deep breath and exhaled slowly as I closed my eyes and pictured the man I married.

"Why Marco? That's all I want to know. Why would you do this to us? To your daughter? You have no idea what you've put us through the past two years. Now to know you've been alive all this time, it makes me want to hate you." I heaved a sigh as I tried to keep myself calm.

"You're an unbelievable piece of scum. You know that, right?"

He rubbed his hands against the knees of his suit pants and stammered over his words. He had to know there would be nothing he could say to make this better. He stood and walked over to me and held out his hand. I gave him my hand and he pulled me up to him.

"Vera, I love you very much, and I am sorry I caused you and Mia so much pain. I really had no other option. I didn't want the cartel to hurt you two because of my stupidity. I was skeptical if it would work or not, but it did. I wanted to come back so many times, but I was afraid that I would get found out and they would come after me. Plus, there's the issue of faking my death being a crime. I wouldn't do well in prison, Vera. I hope you can understand and forgive me."

I laughed in his face as he said those words. I couldn't believe he had actually said that to me. Forgiveness would be the last thing he ever got from me. I wanted him to burn in hell. I bit my tongue to keep from saying so, and pushed him away from me.

"You think I am going to forgive you after what you've done to us? What world do you live in, Marco? You can't do something so horrible to someone you supposedly love and expect them to forgive you just like that. Never mind me and my feelings, but how could you do that to your daughter? How could you just move on and start a new life without even trying to let her know you were alive? I don't understand, and I don't care to." I stepped away from him and pointed toward the door.

"I really am sorry, Vera. I never meant to hurt you or Mia this way. I did what I thought was necessary at the time. If I could go back and do things differently, I would. I can't, though, and I know it will take time, but I do hope you can forgive me enough that I might be able to have a relationship with Mia." He stepped out the door and closed it behind him.

I was overcome with anger, and I followed him out. "Whether or not you have a relationship with her will be up to her. I will not force her to have a relationship with you after what you've done! I wish I had never married you, Marco!"

I stomped back inside and watched from the window as Marco bent down to talk to Mia. He handed her a piece of paper, then hugged her. She hugged the little boy that the woman held and they left. Once their car left the driveway, my emotions took over and I collapsed on the floor, crying hysterically. Mac was the first one back in the house, and he ran to me and scooped me off the floor.

I could see in his face, he was worried about me, but he just held me until the sobs subsided. Brad had been keeping Mia occupied outside and they came in as I stood from Mac's lap. I knew Mia would have questions and I made myself ready to answer them, even if I didn't want to talk about it. Brad made sure we were okay and took his leave. It was just Mia, Mac, and me. I felt awkward around him now that he had seen me at my worst, and I was scared of what he thought of me.

After Marco and the woman left, Brad told me that they lived on the other side of town and I'd probably run into them since I was staying for six months. I questioned whether I wanted to be tortured for the next six months, just to be able to keep the house. I decided I would talk to Brad about giving the house to Mac. I knew I couldn't put myself or Mia through any more pain and staying here would do just that.

I tossed and turned all night until I finally gave up on sleep around five in the morning. I got up and started the coffee pot and made breakfast while Mac and Mia still slept. I watched out the window as Mac emerged from the pole barn and began the morning chores. The horses and cows seemed grateful to see him as he gave them their breakfast. I giggled as one of the horses butted his shoulder with its nose as he gave the other one a sugar cube.

I looked away from the window as Mac made his way to the house. I set his plate on the table and made mine and Mia's. Mac and I were sitting down to eat as Mia walked in the kitchen and sat at the table. We ate our breakfast in silence, and I was surprised she didn't say anything about what happened the day before. Mac finished his plate and gave me the sign for thank you before he headed back outside.

After Mac had been outside for several minutes, Mia put her plate in the sink and sat down beside me. I knew it had to be hard for her to understand what had happened yesterday, and I hoped that it wouldn't negatively affect her as his supposed death had affected me.

"Mom, since Daddy is still alive, does that mean he is going to live with us again? I didn't know when someone died, they could come back like that. I thought I was going to have to wait until I went to Heaven to see him again."

I had no idea what to say to her. Her father had started a new life and hadn't wanted us to be a part of it. I wasn't sure how to tell my bright, happy girl that her father didn't want us anymore.

"No, Mia, I don't think your dad will be living with us. He got mixed up with some bad people and now it is safer for us if your dad stays away. Mia, he didn't really die, sweetie. He pretended to be dead to keep the bad guys away from us. He just didn't tell us that he faked it."

She went to her room to process what I had told her and I cleaned the kitchen. As I washed the dishes, I couldn't help but think about the years I spent with Marco and how it was all a lie. After I finished the dishes, I called Brad and told him of my desire to leave town and asked what would happen to the house. Brad was disappointed that I wanted to leave, but he understood why. I was devastated to find that if I didn't stay, the house would be returned to the bank because my ownership would be revoked.

I decided that I would stick it out, and once it was mine, I would give it to Mac. Then I would leave and never come back. I called Mia's school and had her records transferred so she could start school immediately. Once I was off the phone with the school, I went to her room and told her we were going to be staying a while, and she was going to have to go to school here. Luckily she had thought to bring her backpack and a few school things with her.

Time passed quickly, and before I knew it, the six months were up, and it was almost fall again. Full ownership of the house was mine, and after I packed our few belongings, I handed Mac the keys. His face was covered with sadness as he took the keys from my hand and begged me not to go. He and I had grown very close over the past several months and I was sad to leave him. I couldn't stay, knowing Marco and his new family lived across town. I couldn't go to the grocery store without being worried that they would be there. It was better this way, whether I wanted to believe it or not. I watched as Mac grabbed Mia in a bear hug and twirled her around. I knew his heart was breaking, and I hated knowing I was the reason why. Mia waved goodbye and we got in the car with Brad. He drove us back to our apartment in silence and I knew he thought I was making a mistake.

We walked into the apartment we had shared with Marco, and it seemed cold and empty. I missed the farmhouse as soon as I stepped foot back in the old house. I thought of Mac and how he was doing and wondered if he missed me the way I missed him. Mia and I both wrote him letters, hoping to hear from him, but weeks went by with no answer. I wondered if I had made the right choice in leaving, and if Mac would ever forgive me.

Mac

It had been weeks since Vera and Mia left town, and I wasn't used to them not being here. I expected to see Vera in the kitchen when I came in from morning chores, and I missed Mia hugging me before she left for school. They had both become such a big part of my life, I felt empty without them. The Collins family had given me a family, which is something I hadn't had, and Vera and Mia had made that more complete.

I understood why she wanted to leave, but it still hurt. I had grown close to Vera and I wanted to tell her many times how I felt, but I knew she wanted to leave, and me saying the things I felt would have kept her from doing what she needed to heal from Marco's betrayal. I had gotten letters from them both, but I hadn't been strong enough to reply. I needed to forget them so my heart could heal, but I knew that would never happen. I tried so many things to get them off my mind but nothing worked.

I wondered why I hadn't been good enough to stay for, and my mind always came back to my lack of hearing. I decided that I would have a surgery that my doctor had suggested which might allow me to hear again. I used money from the trust set up for me to pay for the surgery, and the recovery was quite painful. Several weeks after the operation had been done, I knew it had worked. I heard the horses neigh when I was feeding them. Now the only thing I wanted was to hear her voice.

I finally replied to her letter and told her I missed her and wanted to see them both. We began writing to each other, and before we knew it, winter was upon us again. I was giving the horses straw when I heard tires crunching the gravel on the driveway. I turned to see Vera and Mia getting out of the car. I was surprised, and my heart swelled with love when I saw them. Mia ran to me and wrapped me in a hug. She squeezed me like she was never going to see me again. I picked her up and held her tight and she giggled as I spun her around. It was the most beautiful sound I had ever heard. I put her down and looked at Vera with tears in my eyes.

"Mac, I'm sorry I hurt you by leaving. I was so consumed by Marco and what he did to us. I couldn't let you in like I wanted to. I didn't think about what it was doing to you. The truth is I really care about you and I want to come back. Do you think you could forgive me?"

I couldn't wait to surprise her. I had been working with a speech therapist and had learned to talk better now that I could hear.

"You and Mia have the most beautiful voices in the world you know that? Of course I forgive you. Come here, sweetheart."

I pulled her to me before she had time to react and I kissed her deeply. She pulled back from me and grabbed my face in her hands.

"You can hear me? You sound so good! I am so happy for you. I loved you anyway, Mac. I want you to know that. It didn't matter to me whether you could hear or not. You saved me in many ways while I was here before, and I am so thankful for you. I tried to learn sign language, but failed. I was just thankful you could read my lips. Now I want you to kiss them."

I couldn't believe I finally had the family I always wanted and I was happy they came back to me. They made me the happiest I had ever been, and I knew I was going to do what I had to so they would have the best life possible. They were my girls and they always would be. Vera said I saved her in many ways. While I was saving Vera, she was saving me.

Winter Love
Rubi Rose

Summary

Alexis is traveling to the US over Christmas, looking for an adventure and wanting to take amazing pictures when she runs into snowboarder Brad. Will she get more than just pictures?

Biography

I live in Auckland, New Zealand and am a stay home mother of two kids under five.

I never thought about writing until my younger sister one day asked me when am I was going to write my own book. So I thought about it and I gave it ago.

Facebook: https://www.facebook.com/AuthorRubiRose/

Readers Group: https://www.facebook.com/groups/AuthorRubiRosesReadersGroup/

Twitter: https://twitter.com/AuthorRubiRose

Winter Love
Rubi Rose

Chapter One

Sitting at the café with my bestie, having coffee, my mind travels to the fact that I am about to take off on an adventure of a lifetime by myself into the unknown and most beautiful place in their winter.

Aspen, baby.

My thoughts are interrupted by my besties' voice, and eyes boring into mine, she is unimpressed. I try not to giggle.

"Alexis, do you really have to go?" She blows out with so much over the top drama that this time I can't hold my laughter in.

Her eyebrows raise up at me in mock horror.

"Come on, babes, you know how long I have been planning and saving for this trip. I have always wanted a white Christmas, and I can finally have one," I say to her with a smile and an "I'm sorry" look in my eyes. I do feel bad, but, man, a white Christmas. I have always wanted one. It will be a dream come true, but I do feel bad since Nicole and I always do everything together, and this is the first time we won't.

"I know, babes, and I'm happy for you. It just sucks that you are leaving me all alone this summer so you can go to the other side of the world for a white Christmas. I think you're mad, by the way, for giving up the nice warm sun for cold and snow." She pretends to shiver.

Downing the last of my coffee, I say, "Let's go babe, don't want to be late for check-in. It's a pain having to check in two hours before departure on an international flight out of New Zealand. That's two hours of my stomach doing flips and my palms sweating first time on a plane. First time away from all I have ever known.

Grabbing my bags, I head out to the car. The sun warms my face and I take a small look around the place I've called home forever. The beautiful and stunning New Zealand, the sun high in the sky, the clouds so white. The sky is the most amazing shade of blue.

It's definitely going to be hard to say bye to this human who has been my bestie for so long. I can't remember a time where she wasn't with me in all that life has had planned for us. To do this epic trip without her sucks. I know I will be back in a few months, but still, it's going to be hard, and I will miss her overdramatic face.

The drive to the airport was short and sweet. I had time to mold the scenery into my mind and lock away to take with me on my holiday. My bestie was singing to the sounds the whole way, her phone connected to the car stereo with her normal over the top Spotify playlist blaring from the speakers.

Pulling into the carpark, we grab a ticket. There are busy people everywhere. The heat hits you in the face as you exit the air-conditioned car rounding to the boot. She pops it open and I haul my bags from the boot. My bestie grabs me a trolley and we head on in, her arm linked through mine as we make our way to check in.

I check in my bags, taking a deep breath. The lady must see that I'm nervous.

"First time flying?" she asks me.

"Yep, it sure is," I say, holding out my hands, showing her how much they are shaking.

"It will be fine. It's beautiful up there, and you will be safe as houses," she says with a warm smile.

"Thanks," I say back to her as she passes me my passport and boarding pass.

Turning, I grab hold of my besties' hand, and we head for the escalator that takes you to the viewing deck with wraparound glass windows and a small café and bar for some food and a drink before I have to head for the gate.

"Make sure you get some awesome photos and we can FaceTime whenever we can."

I pull out my chair, looking down at the tarmac and planes. I watch the hives of activity of what goes into getting a plane ready for flight.

"Of course, we will FaceTime whenever we can, babes. I am so looking forward to being there, and in this amazing new environment with a whole new world of things I can photograph."

"You're a great photographer, Alexis, and I know you will get some amazing shots." The awe in her voice sends a small chill through me. She knows me so well, she knows that this is my passion and just what I want to do.

My flight is called over the speakers and I squeeze my bestie's hand as we walk toward my gate, butterfly swirling around inside my stomach and nerves creeping up my spine.

I pull this crazy girl into me as tears well in my eyes. Her tears streamed down her face. A pang of disappointment and hurt hit me along with excitement and lust for new experiences and memories. I'm trying to not let it show that I am scared shitless, as she will make it so easy for me to turn around and run away back to the comfort of my boring life.

"Gotta go, Chica," I say into her ear, kissing her cheek. "Catch you on the other side of this adventure."

"See you soon," she says to me. "PM me as soon as you like land and shit, okay?" she bosses out, winking at as I turn and walk down my gate.

"Sure will."

Stepping onto the plane, I am overwhelmed and so nervous. I'm greeted by a super friendly flight attendant who tells me how far down my seat is. It's a window seat, yes... I am stoked about that. Stowing my carry on in the overhead locker, I take my seat, putting my belt on and settle in for a long flight.

I watch as the tarmac starts to move under me and the pilot talks to us, murmuring about the weather and shit. I'm shitting myself as the plane speeds up and we begin a rather fast approach toward the end of a runway. I slam my eyes shut. I don't want to see death hitting me.

After a few moments, I open my eyes and see we are, in fact, not dead. Leaning back, I slip my headphones on and shuffle my Spotify playlist and fall off to sleep.

I wake to a flight attendant tapping my shoulder asking if I wanted anything to eat or drink.

I'm shocked that I actually drifted in and out of sleep for that whole flight, waking once to eat and go to the bathroom. Slipping my belt off, I stand and grab my bag from the overhead locker before making my way off the plane and into the LAX airport. After getting my bags, I head over to customs.

It took ages to get through customs, but luckily, I have a few hours before my connecting flight to Aspen. I pull my jacket and my trackies from my bag. I slip them over my bike shorts and tee before I head over to wait for my next plane.

My second flight has just landed and I slip off my belt and grab my carry on before heading off the plane to grab my check-in bags.

Chapter Two

I can't believe I am finally here. Walking along the glass tunnel from the plane, I see the snow and the people all rugged up. It's freezing, but, hell, yes, my first white Christmas.

Waiting for my bag, I look around. I see families meeting loved ones, and kids with rosy red cheeks and mittens on.

When I retrieved my bags, I put them on my trolley and stop at the cute gift store by the exit. I picked up a map, travel guide of what's hot and places to go, a pair of gloves, and a beanie with fluffy ears to cover my rather cold ones.

The chill hits as soon as the glass doors whoosh open. I shiver, looking left and right for a cab. I spot one and holler the way I've seen on *Sex and the City*. Jumping in, he whizzes through the streets to my hotel fast and efficient and rather polite. I was stoked, walking into the hotel. A bell boy meets me and takes my bags as I check in, and then he shows me to my room taking my bags all the way for me. Now, that's service. He's cute. I smile at him in thanks as he places my bags inside my room. I hand him a New Zealand Tenner since I hadn't had a chance to convert money yet.

I look around my rather sexy, cool room its modern chic whites and blacks with pops of red. Dragging my bag to my room before jet lag sets in, I unpack my suitcase and place my clothes in the drawers. I placed a couple of cute, sexy winter dresses and some heavy winter coats on the hangers in the closet. Happy with how it all looks, I store the suitcase under the bed. Picking up my camera bag, I check to see whether I have all I need, including my key card to get back in my room. I walk from the room, deciding to catch the brilliant bight winter days' sun and snap some pics of this stunning place. Butterflies still swim inside me that I am finally here and actually doing this.

Walking from the hotel, I follow the road down a nice cobbled path, tucking my hands in my pockets. Even with mittens on, it's chilly on my fingers. Before I know it, I have walked to the bottom of the mountain that's not far from where I'm staying. That's handy, I think, as I look up, shielding my eyes from the white powder coasting the mountain slopes which is dotted with snowboarders and skiers coming down and going up on chairlifts. The welcoming sounds of laughter and cheering are warming. This is just where I want to be. I look to the right of the mountain with a few snowboarders who are taking the rails and jumps like pros. This will make for some amazing in-air sport shots for my portfolio. Biting my gloves off, I slam them into my pockets as I unclip the lens cap on my Nikon and adjust the lens. I zoom in and out slightly, snapping some amazing shots. These guys are amazing at what they do. They fly down the slope, over the rails, and jump, performing in-air tricks.

Stopping as they reach the bottom, I pull my camera down and start to flick through what I have taken. The light this time of day is perfect, and the snow is so white with the massive pines. It's the perfect backdrop to some remarkable Arial acts.

Looking up to see if any more are coming down—I wouldn't mind snapping a few skiers—I see the two that I just captured walking toward me, boards in hand. They have taken off their helmets and goggles. If I'm not mistaken, they are walking in a straight line to me, and they look rather furious.

"Hey, little lady, what are you doing taking photos here and of us?"

I look around fast for some sort of sign that says *no photos*. Not seeing one, I answer, even though I feel like I may pass out. Confrontation has never been my thing, nor has scary men with pissed off expressions which look like they could eat me whole.

"Who the hell are you, and why are you standing at the bottom of the slope taking photos?" he snaps.

Again, my body tense and I have seemed to have gone mute. *Idiot*, I think to myself.

Looking down so I'm not looking at his face, I watched as I wiggle my boots in the snow.

"Um, look, well, um, I'm sorry. I didn't know I wasn't allowed to take photos here. I have just arrived and I'm kinda on a working holiday, wanting a white Christmas and some shots for my portfolio. I'm a photographer and, well, when I saw you guys coming down the mountain and flipping like that, I just knew they would make for some of the best action shots, so I couldn't help myself. I can delete them, though, if you would like. Again, sorry." *Alexis, you're rambling on like a school girl with a crush on her teacher.*

"Oh, beautiful, don't sweat it. Sorry for being all loud. Welcome to Aspen," he says to me with a killer smile which makes my knees shake. I'm sure it's not from the cold, either. "Can I take a look, babe, at what you took?" he asks me.

I stutter out an "Ooooo, sure."

My hands shaking, I flick the images back to the start and began to show him and his mate, who are both leaning over my shoulders, watching the images flash by. All I can think is that they smell amazing, all man, pine and snow, as their breath hot and heavy hit the exposed skin behind my ears.

"Beautiful, that's some stellar skills you got there. You're a great photographer."

"Um, thanks." I smile at him nervously, excited that he is liking my shots. "It also comes down to great subjects," I blurt out. Instantly, my cheeks flush red. *That was forward even for you, Alexis.*

"Well, it was nice to meet you, but I better head back to my hotel room now," I say, turning on my heel to walk away.

But I walk the wrong way, crashing into a skier who is walking by. My cheeks then flame to a blaze that will rival any bushfire in the Australian summer.

"You all good, sweetheart," his hand reaches out, grabbing my elbow and steadying me.

"Shoot, yes, thank you." My voice shakes as I try to control my embarrassment.

"Well, babe, see ya 'round, aye?" he winks, leaving the question hanging between us as he walks off.

The whole walk back, I couldn't stop thinking about the hot guy and his snowboarding skills. When I get back to my room, I dig my laptop out of my bag and turn it on then log in. I plug my camera into my laptop and bring up the photos I took.

I love the photos I took of him. He has some stellar skills and some amazing teeth and eyes. Listen to me, I've been here for mere hours, and I'm talking like this about a stranger who I snapped a few shots of, and didn't even get his name. *Lord, Alexis, you're a mess.* Blaming that on jet lag.

Reading through the travel guide to see what's hot and not, I come across a bar. The blue-black lighting the whole wraparound couches and low tales solid glass bar wrapping itself in a circle catches my attention. The focal point of the bar looks like a massive slab of ice. I'm stuffing my face with in-house pizza from room service and make my mind up to shower and head out. I can sleep tomorrow. I'm on holiday, after all.

Chapter Three

Walking into the bar, I see it's pretty busy. Well, correction—it's packed. Like so many people, I feel overwhelmed and panicked as the air grows hot and the liquor mixed with so many different amounts of perfumes and cologne fill the air.

I look around the room and spot the bar, so I start heading in that direction.

I end up losing my footing, feeling my body fall. My hands slam out to break my fall when I come face to face with a brick wall with arms wrapping around me.

Hmmmmm hold up. Wait a minute. This isn't a wall is it? Nope. My neck flares and my cheeks redden. It's a rock-hard chest.

Slowly looking up, I freeze and hold my breath.

"Well, look who it is, the sexy photographer who was taking photos of me doing my air today at the slope." His voice is laced with a sexy undertone.

I'm still frozen and can't get a word out, but that's okay because he continues to talk.

"So, beautiful, are you going to tell me your name this time?" he says, letting me go.

Now that I can breathe again and he is no longer holding me, I can think.

"My name is Alexis, what's yours? You remember me?"

He laughs. God, I love that sound.

"I'm Brad. Of course, I remember you."

He puts an arm around me and leans me toward the bar. "What are you drinking?"

"It's okay, I can get my own drink," I say, not wanting to feel like I owe him anything.

"I'm sure you can, but I would like to buy you one and talk to you about the photos you took of me today"

"Oh, well, um, okay, sure. I will let you buy me a drink,

but only because I took photos of you without asking."

He starts laughing. Great, he thinks it's funny.

"What drink do you want, beautiful?"

"I will just have a glass of chardonnay, please."

"Okay." He turns around and calls out to the bartender, "Katie."

The hot bartender turns around and walks over with a big smile on her face.

"What can I get for you, Brad?"

"The lady will have a glass of chardonnay and I'll have my normal, please."

"Sure, Brad," she says, flicking him a killer white smile.

I feel a pang of jealousy and I hate that I don't even know this guy. But, look at him. He's built like a god, and she is…well, she is stunning with a long, sleek blonde ponytail that sits halfway down her back. She has a long-sleeved gray tee on with the club's emblem on it and tight black jeans and candy apple red high heels. She's banging, and well, I'm me. A plain Jane. I have my blue wash skinny jeans on with a white sweater, a navy-blue scarf, and white converses.

His hand snakes over the base of my spine. A small smile creeps over my face as I look up at him. He is so tall, so sexy, I could lick him and not even feel ashamed.

After we get our drinks, we head over to a table in the corner where it's a little quieter than the rest of the bar.

"So, how long have you been taking photos?" he asks me, casual and cool.

I look up at him. He really means it. He wants to know. The only person who has ever wanted to know about my photography has been my bestie, Nicole.

"Um, well, about five years. I was always found with a camera in hand taking photos of anything I could. Then five years ago, my bestie asked if I could take some photos of her. I never looked back after that."

"Wow, that's awesome. What kind of photography do you do?"

"I'm mainly a book cover photographer, but I love taking photos of different landscapes. I work them in with my photos to make pre-made covers."

"That's so wicked, beautiful," he says with awe in his voice. It feels nice to have someone other than my bestie interested in what I do.

"If you would like, I would love to help you out and let you photograph me boarding, or of me with just my board at the bottom of the slope."

"Really? Um, that would be really cool. Thanks."

He starts laughing at me before saying, "That's okay, babes. I would love to help you with your portfolio and your pre-made covers."

Chapter Four

The days here have been amazing—snow falling around the city, people everywhere, hot cocoa and marshmallows by massive open fires in the ski resorts on the mountains. I watch as small flakes fall outside the massive ceiling to the floor window of my room high above Aspen, cherishing the moment, the sight the sound, and the fact that I'm so lucky to be here experiencing this. Brad also definitely makes it a tad more exciting.

I have seen Brad every day for the past two weeks. He has shown me around and also helped me get some great shots for my portfolio. Also, a few Stella shots that will make some amazing pre-made covers for my group. It has me excited that I will be able to deliver some amazing new action shots from a winter wonderland for authors who follows me.

Walking away from the view that grabbed my attention and held me there for what seemed like hours, I pick up my camera bag and double check that I have everything. Picking up my keycard from my room, I head down to meet Brad. He is introducing me to some of his mates who are letting me take photos of them as well.

I had a great day with Brad and his mates, Anthony, Luke, and Harry. Man, all four of them can board. I remember Anthony from the day I met Brad. He was the guy Brad was boarding with. I also got a few great shots of the mountain to use as the background on some pre-mades.

We all head into the café at the bottom of the slope for some coffee before I say goodbye to the guys.

Getting back to my room, I pull my camera out of my bag and put it on the bed before putting my bag on the floor next to the bedside table. I pull my laptop out and get to work on a new pre-made. I use a photo I took of Luke today as the main image. The whole left side of the photo is just the side of the mountain and on the right is him performing a backside triple cork tail grab. I had no idea what it was until the guys told me after. I put the title as "Midair" on the bottom and up the top, I put "Author Name." On the left side where the book blurb will go, I put the details for getting the cover and how to contact me.

After about three hours, I am finally happy with the cover. I put it up in my pre-made group, adding Luke Modglin as the cover model.

I start doing another new pre-made using one of Brad's photos. I use one of my background photos I took the other day and then add the shot of Brad doing a double cork three sixty. I created the title as "Double Cork" at the top, then wrote "Author Name" at the bottom. After I add my details to where the blurb will be, I upload it into my group as well, adding Brad Wood as the cover model.

Looking at the comments on the pre-made of Luke, I see a few people say they love it. A couple minutes later, I get a message from an author who would like to buy Brad's cover for her upcoming snowboarding series. I let her know I will make up a contract and email it to her in the morning. I ask for her details to add to the contract, which she sends through straight away.

I go back to my post and edit it so it has *sold* at the top. Then I head down to the bar for some food and a drink.

Walking into the bar, I see the guys sitting around drinking and laughing. Anthony sees me and calls out my name. The others turn around.

I order my drink and head over to their table to join them.

I tell them I made a couple of pre-mades from the shots today. One of Luke and one of Brad. Brad's sold within a couple of minutes. They order another round of drinks and we chat about the photos and I agree to add into the contract for the author to send a copy to whichever of them are on the cover.

When I get back to my room, I make the contract and email it off to the author before I head to bed.

I had a quick bite to eat downstairs in the restaurant for lunch. Walking into my room, I head for my laptop to see if my bestie is online for our FaceTime. She is online, so I click the button to call her. She picks up after the second ring.

"Alexis!" She screams, but before I can speak, she continues, "I was starting to think something happened to you and I needed to send out a search party. I haven't heard from you in days. We always talk at least once a day."

"Yeah, sorry, Nicole. I have been busy taking photos of the hot snowboarders I told you about."

"That's okay, babes. How is it going with your hot snowboarder? What's his name again?"

"Brad. Yeah, it's good. We have been out a few times."

"So, are you seeing each other or are you just friends?"

"We are just friends. Brad and his friends are helping me with my photography."

"Yeah, sure, babes, if you say so."

"What is that meant to mean?"

"It means I think you and Brad are more than just friends."

I look away from the screen. Damn it, I forgot she is so good at reading me. I do have a crush on Brad and want to be more than friends, but I only just met him. Not that I will tell Nicole that.

"I am so right aren't I, Alexis?"

We spend the next twenty minutes of me trying so hard to act normal and not cave in and tell her all about my thoughts of Brad and how much I want to be his girl. However, I just can't. She's my bestie, and she knows me better at times than I know myself, so I cave. I blurt it all out—from the butterflies to the giddy feelings and the blushing cheeks to the fireworks when he's around me. I tell her when he grazes my skin in greeting I begin shivering for him to make me his. She begins to scream and coo and vow to skin me if I keep any hotter thoughts and meetings with Brad and the boys to myself. I laugh at her over the top exaggeration of this situation.

"You know, I may just have to come over. These men sound delish," She quips, and I laugh out loud into the phone.

"Gotta go, babe. Photos to edit and covers to make." I hear her sigh.

"Sorry, babes. I miss you and I'll call tomorrow, I promise."

I mouth into the phone, "You bloody better."

She says, "Will do. Bye, doll."

I fall back on the overly too-soft bed and close my eyes, rolling our conversation over in my head as I think of the reality of my omission and how much I like Brad and want to actually be with him.

Chapter Five

I spend the day with Brad, taking photos and having snow fights. Laughter falls easily when I am around him. I am contently smiling and I have to say he makes me feel so alive. I caught him a few times today just staring at me, and I feel the heat creep up not only my cheeks, but also my core. He set a fire in my belly.

As we are wrapping up the day sitting in the lodge at the base of the mountain, my thoughts are in fairyland. I stare into the open fire. Roaring flames lick up over the pine logs, sending a delish scent out over us all.

I jump slightly as Brad's hand runs up the outside of my thigh. My eyes snap to his hand as my thighs clench. I slowly bring my gaze to his.

"Sorry," he mouths to me as I bring the cup of cocoa up to my mouth.

"For?" I say, my voice shaky and not its normal cool self.

"Making you jump, babe."

Ooooo, hell, he called me babe. My cheeks begins to burn. "It's okay. I was away with the fairies," I mouth, placing my hot cup on my knee. His hand is still running small lines up and down my thigh and my body is buzzing.

"Wanna go out for dinner tonight just me and you, babe?" he asks me. I have to swallow the lump that has formed in my throat. We have hung out so much over the last few weeks, but this, well this feels different somehow. It feels romantic.

"Ummm, yes, yes, I'd love that," I stutter, feeling like a fool.

A smile cracks over his face as he leans in. His woodsy and fresh snow smell hits me. I close my eyes and just breathe him in, his lips meeting just below my ear. His breath is hot on my skin.

"Great, babe. I'll pick you up at eight." Before I can answer, or even open my eyes, his lips kiss lightly under my earlobe. I slowly peel my eyes open and see him walk through the massive glass doors, grabbing his board and heading off down the street with the boys in tow.

He takes me out for dinner to a restaurant I didn't know was here. I guess it's a place for all the locals.

The food was great and I am so full now.

He drives me back to my hotel and walks me up to my room. He wraps his right arm around me before he pins me to the hard wooden door. His mouth closes over mine. It starts out slow, then turns to a hungry, passionate kiss. My hair is tangled in his left hand as he sucks on my tongue.

His hand slides down my back, leaving a tingling path where he touched.

It's a good thing Brad has his arm around me and that I am pinned to the door, as my legs have turned to jelly and I couldn't hold myself up.

When he pulls away, we are both breathing heavy.

"Where is your keycard?"

I still can't talk, so I pull my keycard out and hand it to him. He opens the door and lets me in. Before giving the card back to me, he kisses my cheek.

"I better go, beautiful. See you tomorrow."

With that, he closes the door behind him, leaving me alone just inside my room.

Chapter Six

I was going to meet Brad at the slopes. I had asked him to teach me how to snowboard, but he said we have a change of plans as a storm is due to hit about midday and the slopes are closed.

He picks me up from my hotel to head over to his place. I am a little scared because I have never been to his.

"Bring your laptop, camera, and whatever else you need for your photography and pre-made covers. Also, bring a change of clothes just in case we get snowed in since my place is on the edge of the mountain."

"Um, okay." I start getting a few clothes in my duffle bag, enough for a couple days just in case. I grab a few bags of my kiwi treats I brought over from New Zealand and put them in. Then I check that I have my camera, laptop, and everything for them, including my phone charger—not that any of it will be any good if we get snowed in and we lose power. Wait, can that happen?

The car ride over to Brad's was only five minutes from my hotel and we didn't say much.

He pulls off the road and into this long driveway that snakes its way up the side of the mountain a bit.

Oh, my God, the house is gorgeous.

He pushes a button in the car and the garage door opens. He has like four other cars in that huge garage and they are all different.

After he parks the car and turns it off, he pushes the button again to close the door. We get out and he helps me carry my bags up the stairs.

When we get to the top of the stairs, we walk into a huge kitchen and I fall in love right away. It's my dream kitchen, not that I will ever have the money for one. I could get lost in here and never leave.

Shiny black marble tiles that cover the floor matches the

shiny black marble countertops. All the doors are white with shiny silver handles. A huge kitchen island stood in the middle with black bar stools on one side. He has a big double door fridge freezer.

When I look up at Brad, I realize I was acting like a little kid in a candy store. He smiles at me and tells me to follow him through the door, saying the kitchen isn't going anywhere.

We end up in a room twice the size of the kitchen. It has a huge black leather corner couch and a huge flat screen TV which is melted onto the wall with a surround sound system. The whole wall on the left of the TV is floor to ceiling windows with a stunning view of the mountain behind.

"I thought since the storm is coming in, we could watch something, or if you wanted a model to take some shots of that aren't on the mountain or in snow gear."

"We can do a few shots, then watch a movie."

"Okay, cool."

I take a few different shots of Brad. We make a pre-made together with a couple, then the rest I put up for sale on my website. I log off and put my camera and laptop back in their bags. I head over to sit next to him on the couch. When I look over at the coffee table, I see Brad had made some popcorn.

Heading back across the room to my bags, I grab my kiwi treat and a few bags of Pascell's classic kiwi lollies Pineapple Lumps, Jaffas, Jet Planes, and my all-time favorite milkshake. I also got a bottle of lemon and Paeroa (L&P), as well as a few bars of Whittakers L&P chocolate and Whittakers Jelly Tip chocolate. Turning around, I see Brad trying to hide a smile.

Cuddling up to Brad on the couch, he pushes play on a movie on Netflix. I must have fallen asleep sometime during the movie because I wake up and I have a blanket on me and the movie is finished.

"Come on, babe, let's get you to bed."

"Yeah, okay."

Upstairs, we walk into a bedroom and I know straight away it's Brad's bedroom because his stuff is all over the place. We put my bags down in one corner.

I grab my PJs, toothbrush, toothpaste, and head into the bathroom to get ready for bed.

When I come out, he is lying on one side in bed, waiting for me. Putting my dirty washing next to my bag, I hop into bed next to him. He wraps his arms around me and I fall asleep.

TO BE CONTINUED

Acknowledgments

My fiancé, Vernon, thanks for all the support you have given me—with everything, not just my writing. You're my rock and I don't know what I will do without you. I love you xx

My Nana, Beverley Exley, thanks for helping me pick a title for this story, the endless phone calls and supporting me on this writing journey.

Angela Kay, thanks for letting me be a part of this anthology and helping me with anything I needed for my first anthology.

Cynthia Carpenter and Carol Thomas, thank you ladies for being my beta readers and your endless support throughout this journey.

To the readers, thank you for taking a chance on this story.

Frost Smitten
Paige Clendenin

Summary

When high maintenance, Sophy Williams, a businesswoman from New York decided to head into Maine for a high dollar business presentation, she chose to ignore the warnings of an oncoming snowstorm despite the news and reminders from her secretary. All Sophy cared about was the bottom dollar, not the company she was trying to convince to use her services, or the owner of said company.

When Sophy found herself thrown out of the car that had taken her to Maine by a disgruntled driver, she was shocked the snow had blocked the road, and her chances of settling her deal with farmer boy. The driver had escaped with her cell phone, and dignity, leaving her to fend for herself for the first time in her life. Clad with Jimmy Choo shoes, a Parisian cloak, and armed with a briefcase, Sophy was determined to meet the man called Blake Macintosh, even if it meant she had to go the rest of the way on foot, in the freezing cold, with snow falling all around.

When the handsome Blake Macintosh showed up on horseback to save the day, Sophia was put out by his mode of transportation. The cold and impending nightfall made the decision for her. She had no other choice than to go home with farmer boy. Could a week snowed in at an apple orchard with Blake and the little girl called Lilly change a heart that has long been frostbitten?

Read this tale of unexpected change to find out if a heart turned bitter and cold can be warmed enough to allow love to enter in.

Biography

I am Paige Clendenin. I have been married to my best friend, David, for over thirteen years. We have four wonderful daughters, who, along with David, are the inspiration behind my writing. I work hard to enjoy life to its fullest and value family and friends above all. I am passionate about keeping my mind stimulated, imagination running wild, and my dreams coming true.

Links:

Paige's Shared Facebook Readers Group: Two Ladies Magic and Mayhem

https://www.facebook.com/groups/306946713370729/

Paige's Facebook Author Page:

https://www.facebook.com/paigeclendeninauthor

Paige's Twitter

https://twitter.com/paigeauthor

Paige's Amazon Author Page:

https://www.amazon.com/Paige-Clendenin/e/B07GLN27FF

Newsletter Sign Up:

http://eepurl.com/dPdFob

Frost Smitten
Paige Clendenin

Chapter One

I watch out the window of the Uber as the car zooms past other taxi cabs and cars such as this, doing all the same thing...heading in and out of the city. Christmas was only a few days ago and already I am ready to get away. New Year's Eve is only three days away. New York is a hustle and bustle kind of town and New Year's is the worst. Truth be told, if all pans out, I will be done with my trip and plant myself in a spa for a few days and wait out the madhouse that is New York this time of year.

For weeks, we have been knee-deep in the bitter cold snow. I love the city, but the winter is my least favorite part of it. I would say that my trip out of the city is exciting and that I am going to be going on vacation in Tahiti, but I'm not.

I don't much care for the holidays, as I have been spending them all by myself since I was seventeen. That was ten years ago. I came to the United States from my homeland of England on my own when my career had opened the door for me. You might think it is weird that I was seventeen and already had a career, but I was quite the entrepreneur. I had deeply seeded dreams of having an empire in the states, and since the age of twenty-one, I have been ruling my own company.

VastlyOriginal.org is my baby. We take original ideas from people all over the world and set them into action. At first, the company started as a .com, but now I own and operate a forty-story company. That is what is bringing me out of New York today. I am heading to Maine to hold a meeting with a farmer with an apple orchard who thinks he might be able to solve all the problems the apple industry is facing today.

As if there are that many, I'm sure.

Also, as if New York isn't cold enough, let's add the blistering frost-bitten temps those from Maine are accustomed to.

The Uber will take me all the way to the man's house and wait for me there. I know, I know, the trip will nearly take eight hours, but I have the money, and the driver has the time. A win/win I would say.

"Do be sure to take the I-95 up north, dear," I command, "I'm not about to be taken on any backroads."

"Yes, Miss Williams," the driver says to my request.

My name is Sophie Williams, by the way of the Berkshire Williams. My father is a businessman and my mother, an ex-Duchess. You could only imagine the scandal which surrounded that bit of disloyalty…she was married to a duke at the time of my birth, but it was discovered immediately that my mum had been frolicking with his lawyer. I guess I looked too much like my father that it was apparent. Another reason I fled home as soon as I could. My family would never know where to find me—I don't have any intention of telling them my whereabouts any time soon, either.

I have plenty of work to last me the time we will be driving, so I settle down into my Parisian fur lined smock, slip off my Jimmy Choo heels, and take down my hair which slips down my back and falls around my waist in ringlets of chocolate brown.

This might be a long trip, but I plan on making it lucrative and quick.

Chapter Two

I am pouring myself into the presentation I plan on showing farm boy. Men like him are total pushovers and I should have the deal sealed by an hour or two. All I will have to do is bat my eyes and shake my arse at him, as I have done hundreds of times before, and he will be putty in my pretty, polished hands.

My phone vibrates in my lap, startling the bloody hell out of me.

"Hello," I say as I pull up my video chat on my mobile to reveal Chantal, my secretary.

"Sophie, hi." Chantal's meek demeanor plays over the screen.

"Ready for dictation?" I ask.

"Sure," Chantal clamors while trying to find her legal pad.

"You really should be prepared for taking dictation before you call me. Chantal, really, dear, haven't you learned that yet?"

"Ye…yes ma'am."

"Are you ready yet?" I ask with a brisk tone.

"Ready when you are." She tries a smile.

"I'm ready," I say, a bit tired of her antics.

"Case number, purpose of meeting and pitch, and applicant's name?" she asks.

I briefly riffle through my notes on my computer, as I adjust my mobile to prop on the screen.

"Caseload 71605," I begin. "Pitch on my part is to hook him into using our services. His pitch has something to do with apples, and his name is Blake Macintosh, or farmer boy…whichever."

"Anything else," Chantal asks.

"I don't believe so."

"One last thing, ma'am," she says as if not wanting to

say the next part. "They are calling for a winter storm in those regions…you…you might want to cancel the meeting and reschedule for another day once the snow has cleared."

"Reschedule, my arse, Chantal. What in the bloody hell are you thinking?" I am in disbelief. "I will not now, nor ever, cancel a meeting."

"Ye…ye…yes, ma'am," Chantal stammers again as if afraid of me. She then clicks the mobile off and the screen returns to black.

I throw my cellular back down in my lap, bewildered. I can't imagine why she would be afraid of me. Am I that intimidating?

Bewildered over Chantal and thinking who in the world would name a farm boy Blake Macintosh, I allow myself to pull my silk sleeping mask over my eyes and place my head on the back of the seat, hoping to shorten this trip by allowing myself to fall fast asleep.

Chapter Three

A subtle shaking wakes me from my sleep. It takes me a minute to figure out the utter darkness I am seeing is due to the fact I still have my sleep mask on.

"Ma'am," the driver's voice calls out from the front seat. "Ma'am."

"What?" I ask while pulling off my mask. I look out the window and notice that the Uber has come to a stop altogether. "Where are we?" I ask.

"Just outside Manchester, Miss."

"As in Maine?" I ask.

"Yes, Miss."

"Why aren't we just inside of Manchester?" I ask, bewildered by the fact that vehicles have stopped all around us.

"There are snow drifts up the road that will not be cleared for hours now, perhaps days." He says the last part as if he fears that dragon lady might bite his head off at any moment.

I pick up my mobile again and dial Chantal.

"Hello, Miss." Chantal's voice weakly beams through the cellular.

"Yes, could you be a dear and call farm boy's people and ask them to pick me up as close to the drifts outside of Manchester as possible?" I hang up without a response.

She wouldn't dare not to do what I asked. Her job would depend on her compliance.

I get out of the car with great protest from the driver, wrap my Parisian smock around my body as tightly as possible and instruct him to fetch my small luggage from the hatch. I bend over and pile all my documents and computer into my brief, stand up, and hand it to him.

"What is this for, Miss?"

"You are going to carry my things over that pile of snow

up there," I point toward the snow drift.

"I beg your pardon, Miss, but there is no amount of money in the world that would make me do that." He pauses. "It would be nightfall before I could return to my car, and ain't no one getting out of here in the dark."

"But…" I stammer, confused.

"There is no but about it," He tosses my bags to the ground. "I will bill your company, but I ain't going any further with you."

"Fine!" I yell at him as he gets back into the Uber and backs away from me, angrily turning donuts in the snow.

He flips the bird at me as he drives off and I cannot think of a reason why he would do that.

"Damn," I scream. "I left my mobile in your car!"

Either he didn't hear me, or he doesn't care, but he speeds off back toward New York, nonetheless. I owe that bastard a strongly worded letter.

Perhaps a bit more.

I turn around, gazing at the ground where my luggage is in a heap in the snow. I dust it off the best I can and drag it toward the direction of the snow bank, hoping beyond all hope Chantal got ahold of farmer boy.

Chapter Four

I get no further than ten feet when my left heel breaks. I sink into the snow even further than I once was. So much for my little black Chanel dress staying clean.

I reach down and sadly break the other heal off my Jimmy Choo's, almost crying over my eight-hundred-dollar shoes going down in flames. No worries though, I have ten more pairs at my penthouse nearly just like these.

I begin to hike up the hill, but have no luck gaining grip in my broken shoes. Every three feet I gain, I fall back two of them. I am beginning to get frustrated, and for some reason, all I want right now is to catch sight of farmer boy and a dry warm car or talk to Chantal.

After great athletic feats and an arse that hurts like I have been working out for days, I have finally reached the top. I stand, looking over the top of the huge mound.

I look back down the side I had just come from. There are cars filling the space behind the snow drift, even more than there were however long ago that bastard left me. I look down on the front side to nothing at all, not even a track in the snow.

It looks like the people of Manchester got the notice a long time ago and do not even dare try to leave their warm and cozy homes.

"Hey, you," a man's voice calls from off to the right.

I startle and fall the entire distance down the front side of the hill. My luggage and brief tumble after me. I am in total shock at what has just happened. I am so embarrassed that all I choose to do is lay here in the freezing cold snow, hoping that in no way anyone saw what happened.

Lucky for me, I fell on the side where there are no cars, but once I find out who yelled for me, I might just sue them for non-discretionary stupidity. Finally, I sit up to a sight I thought I never would. A man on a horse is riding down off the snow bank, wearing brown work boots, and a matching Carhartt winter coat. I can see from where the zipper is pulled down ever so slightly that he is wearing a red plaid button-up underneath. I cannot help but think I just found farmer boy.

Chapter Five

I look on in disbelief as the man and his horse continue to come in my direction. He looks at ease on the back of the beast and truth be told, I haven't come any closer to one of the animals than looking at them through my Sportster, running down the highway.

"You Miss Williams?" he asks through his deep and husky voice.

"I might be." I try to turn on my charm. What little charm I might have left after falling off a snow cliff. "It depends on who's asking."

"The names Macintosh…Blake Macintosh." He smiles through a perfect set of white teeth.

"Yes," I smile. "I am Sophia Williams…You can call me Sophy, if you would like?"

"Well, Miss Williams," he grins. "If you would hop on, I will get you to the orchard and get you some dry clothes. My sister Lilly's things should fit you just fine."

He eyes my body, most likely sizing me up against his sister.

"I'm not getting on that thing," I say.

"Suit yourself, Miss Williams." Blake begins to turn the horse around. "It's going to be an awfully cold night out here."

"Might you have a mobile I could borrow?" I ask the man.

"A what?" The country bumpkin asks bewildered.

"A mobile," I say frustrated. "A cellular phone? I left mine in the Uber."

"Oh," the man says. "I don't have a cell phone…I never needed one."

"What are you living in…the stone age?"

"Miss Williams, if you are not going to take a ride with me, and insist on insulting me, I will be on my way."

I watch as he leads the horse toward the direction I can only assume is the way of his orchard. I begin to think this man is not bluffing and will leave me out in the cold to freeze my arse off.

"Wait," I yell toward the man and his beast who are now nearly dots in the distance. "Wait," I scream again, this time running toward him as best as I can while dragging my things along with me.

He and the horse stop in their tracks, turning around toward me. He doesn't come back in my direction. He waits for me to catch up to him. I suppose there are no men that are chivalrous left in this world. One kicks me out on my arse, and the other makes me walk like a pack mule.

I think for half a second, I might have the nerve to cancel this meeting after all. I look at my watch to see if I am anywhere near the correct time, as I must be hours late, but my watch is gone altogether.

I must have lost it during the fall.

"I'm sorry, Mr. Macintosh," I say as I approach him. "I would love a ride to your home to perhaps wash up." I look at my hideous outfit.

"Blake." He smiles a bit as he slides off the horse.

Farmer boy…Blake…helps me up on the horse in my very un-modest attempt to mount the creature. Once I am somewhat atop of it, he straps my luggage and brief on with ropes…I have never seen this done in my life.

Afterward, he takes the reins of the horse and goes on, leading us on foot.

"Are you not going to ride as well?" I say, noticing my British accent becoming thicker, the colder I get.

"Lady," he sounds serious. "You don't strike me as the kind of woman who likes to share."

"Usually I do not," I whisper. "I don't mind, though, really."

He looks at me for a moment, perhaps studying if I am

being truthful or not.

"Move up." He smiles. "I didn't much feel like walking ten miles in the snow."

"Ten miles?" I gulp.

He slides on behind me. I can feel the muscles in his upper arms as he wraps them around me, grabbing the reins between his gloved hands.

"Here," he says, handing me an identical pair of dirty old work gloves from his pocket. I slide them on my frost-bitten hands. "Yah!" he yells as he whips the reins against the hide of the animal, and we shoot off toward the sunset, me in the arms of a stranger.

Chapter Six

We trot up in front of a beautiful farm home. The ride, to say the least, was cold, but to be honest, it was much faster than I thought it would be. I had no idea how fast a horse could run in ten miles.

"I have to house him," farmer boy says.

"What do you want me to do?" I ask.

"You can stay here and wait for me, or you can come to bed him with me."

I look around from side to side, realizing that even though we are in front of his beautiful home, there is nothing but snow as far as the eye can see. I don't much want to be alone out here in the middle of nowhere at night.

"I will go with you," I say. "If that is okay?"

"It is." He smiles as he directs both the horse and me around to a stable.

There are other horses in the stalls. Ones that are young and others that are older. Each one of them is so gorgeous. I reach up and pet the snout of a beautiful white one.

"She bites." He snickers when I jump back like a bullet out of a gun.

"You're joking?" I ask aggravated.

"I am." He laughs more. "That one is Honey Bell. She belongs to Lilly. She is kind and gentle."

"Your sister, right?"

"Right!" he says, distracted.

I finish petting Honey Bell while Blake finishes housing our ride.

"What is her name?" I ask, pointing to the horse that brought us here.

"His name is Goliath." He smiles. "This old man is mine."

I reach up and pet Goliath, giving him a bit of attention. Blake takes my luggage and brief after brushing the horse out and putting some more hay in with him and walks toward the door.

"Do you want me to carry those?" I ask.

"I've got it, Miss Williams."

"Sophia...please." I smile.

"Sophia." He returns my smile.

We walk out of the stables as Blake muscles the enormous doors into place. He picks my things back up and leads me to the back door of his house. In the darkened distance, we can hear the howls of wolves.

"They never come up this far," he reassures me.

"I have never heard them before," I admit.

"Have you not ever gone on a rustic vacation? Seen a bear, heard the wildlife?"

"No!" I say. "Spas and villas for me," I finish, now feeling a bit stuck up for admitting that.

Our conversation falls silent as Blake leads me into his house. It is decorated in a very masculine way, which would lead me to think that he doesn't have a wife.

"You're home," a young girl comes running, wrapping her arms around Blake.

He drops my bags and swings the girl in circles.

"See, I told you I wouldn't be gone long."

"B, that woman, Chantal, called ten times before the phone line went dead."

"Shit," Blake swears. "I knew it was only a matter of time."

"Wait, what is going on here?"

The girl then notices me for perhaps the first time since I entered the house.

"When the phone lines go out, the power is next," Blake admits." There is a bad one coming our way...they are expecting all of Manchester to be snowed in."

"The worst snowstorm in ages," the little girl says to me.

"Do you have any torches?"

"Torches?" Blake asks.

"She wants flashlights, B!" the girl responds.

"Oh, right, you're from England."

"That I am." I smile.

"Go off and grab some torches." he looks at me with a smile.

We watch as the vibrant child runs off in search for torches in case the power were to go out.

I don't know what I am going to do. I have no way of contacting Chantal, or anyone else for that matter.

Chapter Seven

I look on as the girl rushes around, readying everything for a storm they don't know for sure they are going to have. Blake leads my luggage and me upstairs and lands my bags on a bed in a spare room. I open my luggage to see what I might be able to change into once I shower, but everything is soaked.

Blake walks out of the room for a moment and then comes in carrying a white nightgown and some panties which must belong to his sister he said was named Lilly. I wonder where she is.

"You can use the shower at the end of the hall." He smiles. "There are towels in the basket to the left. I will throw your things in the wash before the power goes out."

He leads me to my shower with all my clothes in hand.

"I will hand my clothes out to you." I smile.

I undress in the bathroom, wrapping a towel around me. I hand my wet dress, bra, and panties to Blake, so he can wash them for me. I can hear him stomp off. I get in the shower and let the heat of the water washes over me. Once I feel like I am all clean, I get out and towel dry.

I suppose towel drying my hair is the only option I have as I look around the bathroom to find a dryer and realize there isn't one. Once dry, I slip the gown over my naked body. The cotton slips down my torso and rests, exposing half my arse.

His sister, Lilly, and I are nowhere near the same size. I take the gown off and look at the number on the tag. It is a ten-twelve kids. What is this guy thinking? I don't even try on the panties...no way I'm going to fit into those.

"Blake!" I holler out of the door, hoping my voice carries down the steps.

"Coming!" he yells back up to me.

I can hear his footsteps coming toward me.

"What's wrong?" he asks through the bathroom door.

"Do you have something to tell me about Lilly?"

"Clothes too small?"

"You might say that!"

"I will get you something of mine," he whispers as he walks off.

As Blake walks off, I fold the gown back up, wondering how he could have been so off.

"I hope these will work," he says as he hands me ball shorts, a Luke Bryant T-shirt, and a pair of new boxers. He also included a shiny hairbrush that says *unicorns are real* on the back of it and a pink sparkly elastic band.

I hand the gown and panties back to him, closing the door behind me. The boxers are a bit big, however the shorts have a drawstring on them, so they fit just fine. The shirt is three sizes too big, but it feels comfy. I walk out a few minutes later with the brush and elastic in hand. My hair hangs in long wet waves down to my hips.

I walk downstairs to meet Blake and the little girl.

"Can I brush your hair?" The child beams.

"No," Blake begins to protest.

"It is fine." I put a hand up to him. "She can brush my hair."

I sit on the floor, cross-legged, and let the girl brush through my hair. It feels good to have someone do it for me. She puts it in a long braid and fastens it with the elastic at the end. I stand up and give her a hug.

"Could I trouble you for a pair of socks?" I ask Blake.

"I will get them for you Sophy," the child says as she runs off.

"I like her," I smile. "She has got spunk. Do you know how long it has been since I have been around children?"

"Do you know how long it has been since she has been around a woman?" He frowns.

"A while?"

"Since our parents died," Blake frowns. "They have been gone for nine years. I was nineteen when they left to go home, and Lilly was only one," he pauses. "I have taken care of her since. She just turned ten, and I am the only family she has."

"Sophy, I picked you pink ones!" She hands me a pair of pink fluffy house socks.

"Thank you, Lilly," I say as I hug her.

I feel like I might have just made a new best friend in a ten-year-old.

Chapter Eight

Lilly begins to yawn the second the washer goes off. I can tell by the look in her eyes, she is fading fast.

"Do you want to switch the laundry?" Blake asks, "Or do you want to put Lilly to bed?"

"I can put her to bed if you want." I smile.

Blake looks at me, shocked by my choice. Lilly beams as she pulls me up off the ground. I then follow her to her *My Little Pony* bedroom, where I stay just outside her door, to give her privacy to change into her pajamas. She comes out wearing pajamas matching the theme of her room.

Lilly grabs my hand and pulls me over to her bed, where she plops down on it, dragging me with her. I sit next to her as she snuggles down into the covers.

"How long do you think you are going to be here, Sophy?" Lilly asks me innocently.

She must really be needing some female attention.

"I don't know," I admit. "How long do you want me to stay here?"

"Forever," she giggles.

"I don't know about forever, but perhaps a few days, or at least until the snow drift clears."

"Can you sing to me?" she asks through a series of yawns.

"I don't sing," I admit.

"Sure, you do," she looks at me. "Everyone can sing."

"Not me," I shake my head.

"Okay," she mock pouts. "Maybe next time."

"We will see." I smile as I catch myself hugging her.

I haven't known this child or her brother very long. It confuses me how much one little girl can melt my un-meltable heart. I sit in her room for a while as she drifts off to sleep, admiring how precious she looks. I can't remember a time when I was so young. To think about it, that wasn't long ago. It makes me sad to think I missed out on being a child because I resented my childhood.

In the distance, I can hear Blake shut the dryer door, clicking the appropriate buttons after.

I walk out of the room, turning the lamp off on my way, shutting the door behind me. Two steps out of the room, and the entire house goes black.

"Blake!" I scream, second-guessing my choices, because Lilly is asleep.

I feel along the wall, going the direction toward the kitchen, happy Lilly's room is on the ground floor.

"Where are you?" Blake's voice booms through the house as I see the first glow of lantern light.

"I'm in the hall." I smile as I see his face glowing.

"Is Lilly asleep?" he asks.

"Yes," I smile.

"Well, your clothes didn't get dried...we can hang them in the bathroom upstairs if you would like?"

"Sure," I say.

I walk with him guiding me with his lantern, hoping I can get my hands on a torch in case he and I get separated.

I grab a torch off the table as we pass it. Blake leads me into the laundry room, where he piles my arms up with wet clothes. He takes an equal pile and passes me up, leading me back up the steps to the bathroom at the end of the hall, his lantern hanging from one finger.

Blake drops the pile on the floor as he goes off to find some hangers, me thankful for my torch. I flip it on and its beam illuminates the entire room.

I begin to turn my clothes right-side-out as I ponder the events of the day. I started off in my favorite heels and in an Uber sure to make a buck off farmer boy, just to end it in his home...in his clothes...hanging wet laundry...in his bathroom. I couldn't have guessed I would ever be put in a situation like this, but I can't say I don't like the solitude, division from the hustle and bustle of city life. I never thought I would like it one bit, and had the events of the day gone the way I planned, I would have missed out on the chance to experience it…I mean, really experience it. Sure, I would have seen the apple trees, and the land, but I would not have really seen it. I would have been looking at it all through blinded eyes.

Blake walks back into the room with hangers in hand. He silently begins to hang my wet clean clothes. I join in, not saying a word for a while, but the silence is deafening.

"Will you show me your apple trees tomorrow?" I ask.

"Sure, I can," Blake smiles looking up at me. "I can show you my plans too for your company," he offers.

"We don't have to do that," I say. "I just want to look at your orchard and see what it's like. I have never seen an apple orchard before.

"Something tells me you haven't seen much wild beauty before."

"You're right," I shamefully admit.

"Why all uppity?" Blake smirks.

"I don't know…I just woke up one day and I was like this," I frown. "I don't know why I am so cynical and hard."

"I bet one day on the farm will soften you up a bit," Blake's smile stretches from ear to ear, making his eyes twinkle with excitement. "The trees are dead for the season, but they are still nice to look at."

"Would Lilly like to come with us?" I ask.

"Sure, we could take Goliath and Honey Bell with us too."

"I don't know about the horses so much." I look down.

"I will teach you," Blake offers.

I nod as we do the rest of the hanging in silence.

I wander into my perspective guest room and pile into the bed. I lay in the dark all snuggled under the down-filled covers, happy for the warmth, excited for the adventure that lay ahead of me. Sleep finds me quickly as it pulls me to its actuality with sweet dreams of apples, Lilly, and Blake filling every sleeping moment of the night.

Chapter Nine

The sun shines into the sky, waking me up to a cold, unlit house. I listen for the sounds of someone moving about, but all I hear are the sounds of the fallen snow. I get up, wondering if everyone is still asleep. As I get up, I stretch my arms into the air, arching my back as I feel pops trickling down my spine.

I slip my pink fuzzy socks back on my feet as I tiptoe down the hallway, softly walking the steps to the lower level. When I reach the bottom, I crack open Lilly's bedroom door to expose a made bed, with Lilly nowhere in sight.

After walking into the kitchen, smelling the breakfast waiting on the stove top, I realize for the first time that I am starved. It has been over twenty-four hours since I have put anything into my system. I would never eat the food sitting here if I were back home, subbing egg whites and tofurkey jerky for the bacon and eggs that are fixed.

"Sophy," Lilly beams as she walks into the back door, dressed in warm clothes and a coat that makes her look like a marshmallow.

"Hi, Lilly," I smiled. "Where is Blake?"

"He is out readying the horses." She smiled as she popped a piece of bacon in her mouth. I do the same.

"For us?" I ask through a half-masticated piece of meat.

"Yeah." She smiled.

"Good morning, ladies," Blake beams as he saunters into the room from outside.

He has the same coat on from last night and a rope of some kind over his shoulder. I laugh as I notice the tall rubber boots he has in his hand that match the ones on his feet. I look down at Lilly's feet and notice she is wearing pink ones that are the same as his.

"Am I supposed to wear those?" I ask with a snicker.

"Unless you want to freeze your butt off." Lilly laughs

too.

"I hardly think the heels and little white workout shoes you brought with you will do you any good on a horse in the snow." Blake smiles as he pops a piece of bacon in his mouth.

We all sit and eat breakfast together. I eat more than I know I should and think to myself how I might need to use those workout shoes when I get back to New York. For the first time, though, the thought of going back to New York makes me feel just a little bit sad.

"I put something out in the bathroom for you to wear," Blake says between bites. "I didn't see anything of yours that would be suitable to wear in this blistering Maine weather."

"This should be interesting," I say as I stick my plate in the sink. I pick my ugly Camo green, rubber boots up and head for the bathroom.

When I open the door, I drop the boots, causing a thud to echo through the house.

"Everything alright?" Blake yells up the steps.

"I think so," I sigh.

In front of me is something that makes me both happy and want to crawl into a hole. Blake has been so kind to fold all my dried clothes and place them in a basket that rests inside the small bathroom, but beyond that are the ugliest pair of coveralls I have ever seen.

I take the ugly brown coveralls and pull them up over the shorts and shirt I have on. I cringe at the feel of the not quite burlap feeling rubbing against my made for silk skin. I fasten the straps over my shoulders and put on the massive man's coat sitting next to it. Next, I pull on the hat and gloves placed neatly on the side of the tub. Lastly, I put on the boots, two-sizes too big for me, and wince at my reflection in the full-length mirror on the back of the door.

I clod down the steps, making as much noise as I can to prove my point of protest. When I reach the bottom, Blake is standing in the doorway of the kitchen laughing at me every step I take.

"Oh, shut up." I laugh at him as I playfully shove him on my way by.

Chapter Ten

When I walk outside, I see Lilly already on Honey Bell, just behind Goliath and one other horse I remember seeing from the stable, but don't know the name of. I walk up to the nameless beast and put my fingers in its main. It neighs at me with a slight head bob, causing me to back up a bit.

"Mini is a good horse," Blake says, walking up behind me. "No need to be afraid."

"Mini," I smile as I walk closer to the horse.

I continue to stroke the black and white painted horse as Blake comes up behind me, handing me the rope he had over his shoulder. He shows me how to prepare Mini to be ridden. We put the saddle on her followed by her reins. Blake takes a small piece of rope and ropes Mini to the back of Goliath.

"What is that for?" I ask.

"Mini will stay in pace with Goliath as long as she is tied to him." He points between the horses. "As long as that rope is there, Mini will not listen to your commands."

"I see," I say, happy for the security, but doubtful.

"Now, when you feel safe on Mini and know some basic commands, I can unleash you…but only when you are ready."

He leans down to check one of the shoes on Mini, rising back up, bringing him face to face with me. The air between us circles in cold bolsters mixed with hot breaths. For the longest time, the thickness between us makes time stand still. I notice him…the real him. I hadn't seen how handsome he was until now.

"Are we going?" Lilly breaks the silence, "Or are you two going to stand there looking at each other?"

The smile on her face feels devious and knowing, yet soft and hopeful at the same time.

"We are going," Blake shakes his head. "Now give me your foot."

He reaches down to knee level and cups his hands, awaiting my foot. I place my rubber booted foot into his hands and use my free leg to boost myself up onto Mini.

"That was easier than I thought," I victoriously cheer.

"None of it is all that hard," Blake pats the horse.

I watch him mount his horse, and with a small "yaw," we are in motion. Lilly stays up next to me for the duration of the trip. I take in the splendor of the fallen snow and the apple trees. They are dormant for the season, but the rows of them set in the land look amazing. Miles of land covered in silent snow sends a smile across my face as we leave nothing more than horse hoof prints behind us.

"This is beautiful in the summer." Blake smiles, as he looks back at me.

"I should come back and see it," I say before thinking.

"That would be great." A very excited little girl lets out a squeal.

Blake spends the next few hours teaching me some basic horse maneuvering techniques. Surprised, I have some of it mastered enough to ask to be set free. Together, the three of us, run our horses at a pace equivalent to a brisk walk. My smile is so big my face, it hurts. We stop midday to eat a surprise picnic Lilly had packed for us. Blake and I are both pleasantly surprised as we are both starving.

For some reason, I don't want any of this to end. I may have only known Lilly and farm boy for a day, but it feels like I have been a part of their lives forever.

When we ride back up to the house several hours later, we are all cold and tired.

I dismount Mini and begin to lead her to the stable. The sun is barely hanging on in the sky. We brush our horses together and give them the hay they need. I feel like Mini and I have bonded, which feels strange since I hadn't touched one of the creatures for the first time until last night.

"I love you, Mini," I whisper as I kiss her nose.

"She is something, isn't she?" Blake says as he walks up.

"She is," I admit.

I look over to the other side of the stable to see Honey Bell housed, and Lilly asleep in a pile of hay.

"We must have tired her out," I say.

Blake looks over toward his sleeping sister and laughs.

"She always falls asleep after a ride," he snickers, "Hell, she would sleep out here in the summer if I would let her."

I laugh as I notice again how handsome Blake is. I turn to look at Mini before I blush.

"I would love to have a horse like her someday," I admit.

"She's yours," Blake says automatically.

"What?" I squeak.

He looks down for a second as if he is ashamed. He has forgotten I am not a part of their world.

"I mean for as long as you are here," he corrects himself.

"I would love that," I whisper.

Blake moves in closer to me as I take a deep breath. His manly musk wafts in the air, mixing with my heartbeat that has suddenly become audible.

A moment suspends between us where time again stands still. Snow falls just outside the mouth of the open doors of the stable, sending a shiver down my spine. Blake steps in further, reaching up toward me. He touches the top of my head slowly, bringing back a piece of hay that must have been stuck up there.

"You had this in your hair," Blake says softly as he drops the hay to the ground.

"Oh no," I run my gloved fingers through my hair. "I must look a mess."

"Stop," he grabs my hand. "You look beautiful."

"You think I look beautiful?" I ask as I look Blake in the eye.

"I do," he breathes as he moves in closer.

"Hmmm," I mumble absent-mindedly.

Blake pulls my hand closer to his chest as he gazes at me. I look at him, seeing him see me differently than any single person ever has. The moment lags on as nervous energy flows in and out of me.

"Can I kiss you?" Blake asks me, ever the gentleman.

"Please," I breath as our lips meet.

The heavy moment of our passion pulls at us both. I don't know what is happening to me at all. Who am I becoming?

Chapter Eleven

Blake and I walk hand in hand back into the farmhouse with Lilly, still sleeping, slumped over his shoulder. We tuck her into bed together using a lantern because the power is still out. Blake and I sit down at the kitchen table and talk about our lives. He tells me his parents died in a car accident. Both he and Lilly were at home…Blake was babysitting for his parents while they went for a quick trip to the store…they never returned. I felt bad for him, but in the end, I knew he was a strong man. He would have to be to take care of a one-year-old at the age of nineteen.

I told him a little about my family and coming from England, but he was surprised that I hadn't spoken to them for ten years. He tried to encourage me to at the very least call my mother and let her know I was alive, but I wasn't ready for that.

I fall asleep in my bed in Blake's home, wishing somehow none of this would ever come to an end. I wonder if somehow, I am dreaming it all, but deep down, I know I am awake, and for the first time in years, happy.

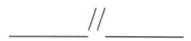

Five days have passed and still no sign of the snow stopping or melting. The power is still out and phone lines are down…probably will be for a while still yet. Lilly and Blake have taken me on more adventures with Mini, Goliath, and Honey Bell, showing off the rest of their land. I got to see some wolf tracks, which both scared and excited me. I loved seeing them, but I don't think I want to ever see the animal that put them in the snow. Each night, we have played board games and made entertainment for ourselves, me having perhaps the most fun I have ever had in my life.

Things between Blake and me have been weird, though.

We haven't kissed any more, but deep down, we both know I will be going home soon. I know I will have to return to New York and leave them behind. There would be no way he would move Lilly into the city and leave all of this for me.

Lilly and I, on the other hand, have grown to be great friends. We have done makeovers and played together. We cooked for Blake last night, and after picking eggshells out for a while, he rather enjoyed my take on scrambled eggs.

The sun is in the sky as I stretch for the morning. I don't know what the day will hold, but something feels different. I don't know what is off about it, but I can't hear the snow fall. I look out the window to see the white ground, but indeed, the snow stopped coming down at last. I run down the stairs to join Lilly and Blake for breakfast, happy for the gas stove we have been using for heat and to cook on.

"I have a serious question for you two," Lilly asks, sounding a bit nervous.

"What's that, sweetheart?" Blake says as he reaches over and ruffles her hair.

"What is going to happen when the snow melts?"

"What do you mean?" Blake asks.

"What is going to happen when the snow melts?" she asks again. "Is Sophy going to go back to New York...or staying with us?"

"Honey," Blake protests. "Why would Sophy stay with us? She has a big business and people she cares for in New York."

I feel bad as I try to think of one person I really care for back home. Chantal is the only human I interact with on a daily basis, and I can't say I have been all that nice to her. I begin to feel bad for how I have treated her. What is wrong with me? Why am I feeling the way I am?

"I don't have that many people back home, really." I look down and then back up at the girl I care so much for. "But I do have a business I love...well, I think I love."

"If you don't know if you love it, then why can't you stay here?"

"Lilly!" Blake scolds her.

"I'm sorry, B." She looks down.

"It's alright." I smile at her as I give her a hug. "I don't really know why I want to go home, other than I have a lot of responsibilities."

"I understand," Lilly says, "but I am going to miss you."

I can see the disappointment in both of their eyes. I don't want to crush them like this at all, but I don't know how I could up and leave the empire I have built just like that.

I can admit one thing, though, although I would never say it out loud, because I don't want to tease myself or anyone else, but I love Lilly so much, and I think I am falling in love with her brother.

Chapter Twelve

After breakfast is cleaned up, we decide to play a game of Twister. I hadn't played it before, but it looked fun. Lilly and I start to twist around each other as Blake calls out body parts and colors. I am in a near backbend over Lilly when she gets right-foot-red called out to her. She tries to move her foot, but ends up tumbling to the ground.

"Ah, man," she giggles. "My turn to call."

I look at Blake for the first time, realizing I am going to be as close to him as I was the other night in the stables. A few minutes pass and we have been tangled all up on the game mat. His handsome eyes staring at me. We laugh together as more and more changes are made to our positioning. Joy flows between us as I can feel the same thickness in the air from a few nights ago.

I can feel Blake inch closer to me, but Lilly being with us causes him to back away. I can tell he wants to kiss me, and I want to kiss him too.

Mid-game, and mid-emotional overload, a loud noise begins to make itself closer to the house. I fall to the ground as Blake falls on me. We jump up and throw our shoes on as we run outside. A huge helicopter is landing in the backyard.

"What in the world is that doing here?" Blake asks.

"Cool," Lilly says as she comes out behind us.

"Sophia," a voice comes from the craft as its door opens.

"Chantal?" I question as I see my assistant climb down and walk my way.

Lilly, realizing who Chantal is from the numerous phone calls she had answered from her before the phones went dead the night I got here, runs into the house crying. I want to chase after her, but I know why she is crying, and I feel like doing the same myself.

"I am here to take you home," Chantel stutters, as she looks at what I am wearing.

"Alright," I say as I drop my head. "Let me get my things."

I turn and walk into the house, feeling Blake right behind me. When I open the kitchen door. Lilly has my luggage and brief waiting for me.

"Go ahead and leave," she yells at me, obviously angry. "Go ahead and leave me and B alone…again."

"I will be back," I try to assure her.

"No, you won't," Blake says from behind me.

"Why do you say that?" I ask.

"Because you will get back to New York and forget about us…once your feet hit the ground, it will be work as usual."

Lilly runs out the door. I can see through the window that she is headed for the stables.

"Blake," I say. "This is my life…will you go with me?"

"I can't," he looks at me with sorrow in his eyes. "You know that I have Lilly to worry about."

"I do," I look down at my hands. "I'm sorry for asking, but I care for you…I care for both of you."

Blake brings my face back up so my eyes can meet his. He leans in and kisses me with passion, for what feels like several minutes. When we pull apart, his eyes glisten with tears.

"I will always remember you," he says as he goes out the door to look for Lilly.

I carry my things out toward the helicopter with tears in my eyes. A man jumps down and loads my things onto it. I then follow Chantal on board as the pilot readies the engine.

Chapter Thirteen
Blake

I can't believe she is leaving. I knew it would happen, but I hoped I would have a few more days with her. I love her…I just didn't want to tell her, because I didn't want her to feel like she had to stay. I would never want to hold her back like that.

I sit down beside Lilly in the stable on a pile of hay, taking her up in my arms as she cries on me. We listen together while the propellers of the craft begin to lift it off the ground. From where we are, we can't see it fly off, but that may be what is best for Lilly.

I know she will be sad for a while…hell, I will be sad for a while, but life was good before Sophia Williams, and it will be just fine after her. We listen as the helicopter gets further and further away, until we can't hear it any longer.

"We need to go in," I say to Lilly. "You don't have a coat on, and it's cold out here."

"Oh…kay," she says through sniffles.

I get up, helping Lilly up after. I hug her tight, and then turn to walk back to the house. I take her hand as the bitter cold wind whips around us.

When we get to the back door, I listen one last time for the helicopter, hoping Sophy had decided to come back, but little to no sound booms through the air.

When I open the back door to go in, I am caught off-guard by the sight before us.

"Sophy!" Lilly yells as she runs into the woman's arms.

Her luggage is sitting at her feet. She is standing in my kitchen with a big smile on her face.

"I couldn't leave," she says.

I run up to her and sweep her up off her feet, spinning her around in a hug. I kiss her softly, despite Lilly's presence. I notice the huge smile on Lilly's face as I put Sophy back down on her feet.

"Are you sure?" I ask.

"I couldn't leave Mini," she joked.

"Oh, sure, stay for the horse," Lilly teases.

"I couldn't leave either of you either." She smiled. "I will send for my things so I can live here. And I asked Chantal to run the company for me…I mean, if you will have me?"

I look at Lilly.

"We will have you." Lilly smiles. "We will have you!"

We all exist blissfully happy, unsure of the future, but I do know one thing…if Sophia Williams will have me, I plan on making her my wife.

Thunder Makes Me Cry
Deryn Pittar

Summary

Fear and confusion reign when Antonia Prebble meets Andrew Mason in a thunderstorm. Not the most auspicious beginning for a romance, which stumbles and falls when Antonia discovers Andrew has lied to her. She decides to continue with her career, leaving Andrew in a position of weakness, something a man in his position is not used to. He wants her forgiveness, but first he has to find her, then he has to convince her to trust him. But he has memories that affect his behavior. Can Antonia be the one to unfreeze his emotions and unlock his heart?

Biography

Deryn Pittar writes romance (contemporary and paranormal), Sci-Fi, Young Adult, Fantasy (think dragons), cozy mystery and short stories. She also dabbles in poetry and flash fiction. She lives in New Zealand, only a click away from the rest of the world.

Her stalker links are:

Amazon Author Page: https://www.amazon.com/-/e/B00JAEN1GW where her published books are listed.

https://www.facebook.com/profile.php?id=100000354971548 personal posts

and www.facebook.com/derynpittar author page

Tumblr: http://derynpittar.tumblr.com for poetry and news

Twitter: https://twitter.com/@derynpittar

Thunder Makes Me Cry
Deryn Pittar

Chapter One

The lights flickered, then dimmed and the glasses on the credenza tinkled. Not a good sound considering she was on the eighth floor. Was the building swaying? Fear raced up her spine and wrapped around her throat in a tight band. She gagged and her legs weakened. The floor came up to meet her. A loud rumble bounced off the plate-glass windows. Her breath faltered and wheezed its way past the lump in her throat.

The boardroom table seemed as long as a cricket pitch. She knew it wasn't, but that didn't help as she crawled along the carpet toward the doorway. A pair of shoes appeared in front of her, attached to smart tartan socks that disappeared up into a pair of bespoke jean legs. She didn't recognize the brand stitching on the sides. She had better things to think about.

"Going somewhere?" A man's voice battered against her thoughts.

Antonia sat back on her heels, straightened her jacket in an effort to retrieve her image. "I'm going to the stationery supply cupboard."

"On your hands and knees?"

"I dropped a pencil. I'm looking for it." She felt around the floor with one hand to embellish her lie. Her fear of thunder and lightning fought for supremacy over her desire to appear as professional as a personal assistant to the senior partner of a law firm would be. Who was this man? She stood by holding on to the nearby chair and then moved to stand with her back against the wood paneling that wrapped the boardroom in a three-sided embrace. In front of her the long glass wall of windows showed the approaching storm. Not a view she wanted to look at. She clamped her jaw shut to prevent an internal whimper escaping. With an effort of great willpower she met the gaze of the intruder who now stood in front of her. At least he blocked the terrifying view. She risked a ragged breath.

"And who, may I ask, are you?" She knew she sounded pompous and should be more polite but fear eroded her usual professional tone.

He returned her gaze, his eyes smiling, a hint of arrogance about his stance. "Just a passing flunkey; I thought I'd fill the water jugs and check on the paper and pencil situation. We might need some more if you've lost one already." His flippancy annoyed her.

Unable to admit her lie, she looked around, avoiding the view through the glass. Her gaze skittered over the long table as she checked the layout. Water jugs and glasses were set at intervals. Small notepads and pencils were strategically placed in case any of the directors needed to take notes. Most would have a phone they would normally put notes into but the chairman, her boss, might insist they leave their phones outside the room. He hated the thought of the proceedings being recorded. Today's meeting concerned a proposed merger with a smaller law firm upstate and the legal intricacies required.

She looked back at the intruder, tall and good looking in a rugged sort of way. His slightly crooked nose might be the result of a punch-up – or a sporting injury. His casual attire ruled him out of the role of board member. Besides, only a secretary or junior assistant would be arranging stationery and filling water jugs.

She opened her mouth to speak when a flash of lightning lit the room like a mega-star. A clap of thunder bounced against the glass a split second later. She screamed and ran from the room, across the hall and wrenched open the door to the supply room. She fell through the doorway, pulling the door shut behind her and huddled in the only empty corner, next to a steel filing cabinet. With her fingers in her ears and her lids closed tight she wept. Terror overwhelmed her like a tsunami. After a lifetime of being scared of lighting and thunder it never got any better. She didn't hear the door open, but sensed movement in front of her. Through tear-filled eyes, she looked up.

He'd followed.

Now he crouched, his gaze level with her. "Do you know the old saying 'If you see the lightning it's missed you; if you hear the thunder, then the lightning has gone—and if you don't hear either you've probably been hit and won't know it."

She sniffed and searched for a tissue or handkerchief. Neither. No pockets in today's outfit. He handed her a white handkerchief. "Keep it. You look as if you need it."

"Thank you," she managed. Through the open door, she heard a distant rumble and flinched.

"It's moving away to the south. It'll be gone within ten minutes." He sounded confident, but what did he know about thunderstorms?

She raised her eyebrows.

"Believe me," he said, "I study of weather patterns. It'll be gone shortly." He offered his hand and pulled her to his feet. His grasp was warm and firm. A shiver ran through her and he put his arm around her shoulder, murmuring as if she was a frightened animal. It sounded comforting and she took a long breath to steady her emotions.

A loud harrumph sounded and the Head of Compliance stood in the doorway, his portly frame almost blocking the light from the passage. She couldn't see his face, but his tone expressed his displeasure.

"Really, Miss Prebble. Fraternizing in the supply cupboard is something I thought temps would do, not Judge

Harding's personal assistant."

She ducked her head, embarrassed and not prepared to explain why she was in the embrace of a complete stranger in the supply cupboard. "Thank you," she whispered to her supporter and fled, sliding around Mr Juckland and hurrying down the passage to the restroom to repair her makeup before she returned to her small office and the pile of correspondence to be processed.

The screen of her computer welcomed her with a display of fireworks as it always did after an absence and she navigated the series of passwords until she found the dictated files she'd abandoned earlier.

Her rescuer had been right. By the time she'd entered the computer system the sun was shining through the windows and white clouds scudded across the gray sky. The autumn storm had passed from sight, probably bouncing its way across the cityscape drenching any poor souls caught out by its sudden arrival. She didn't look at the view very often. Too distracting and dreamy and not conducive to efficient work ethics. She'd moved her desk and put her back to the view when she took the job six months ago having found within several days that she would stop and daydream if she looked out over the city. Her homesickness could be overwhelming at times, but it had an internal fight with her ambition. At the moment her desire to succeed smothered any sneaking regrets that dared to rise in her thoughts.

A chat message flashed on the side of her computer screen. Mr. Juckland wished her to come to his office at 3.p.m. For a moment her heart sank, but once she relived those scary moments in the boardroom she decided she'd done nothing wrong, except for hiding in the supply room. Perhaps the Head of Compliance simply wanted to congratulate her. She'd work some long hours in the last month. He might even offer her a raise. Dreams are free. At least by the afternoon, her puffy, crybaby eyes would have returned to normal. Red-rimmed eyes did nothing for her looks when paired with her auburn hair and freckles.

Damn the thunderstorm.

She took several deep calming breaths and settled into the backlog of court papers Judge Harding needed for a hearing in two day's time.

She rapped twice on the glass. At Mr. Juckland's muffled 'come in' she entered. At his pointed direction she took the chair opposite him. His imposing desk kept him at more than an arm's length from anyone and she wondered if he purposely kept staff and clients at a distance. A sort of power display - 'I'm in charge. You can't touch me'.

Expecting crosswords, she braced herself, determined to be strong and defensive. Instead he smiled.

"Are you feeling better, Miss Prebble?"

She nodded. "Yes, much better, thank you." The need to explain became overwhelming and she rushed on. "I've always been frightened of thunder. It makes me cry. Has done so since I was little…and I didn't ask that man to follow me into the supply room. He just came." Hearing the tumble of her words she stopped and held her lips together. Everything she had planned to say and do now rendered useless.

"That's quite all right, Miss Prebble. I've been informed of the situation prior to my arrival. Do you know the gentleman's name?"

"No, we never got to first name terms, or surnames for that matter."

Mr. Juckland lowered his chin and looked at her from under bushy eyebrows, totally opposite to the light shining on his bald head. It didn't help his efforts to look stern and she suppressed a smile. "I presume from his casual dress and the very fact he was arranging stationery and water glasses that he must an intern at one of the legal firms involved in the merger. I have no idea who he was – or is. Does it matter? Should I know?"

Mr. Juckland almost smiled. A quick lift of one corner of his mouth before it settled into its usual line of disapproval. "No, Miss Prebble. It's of no consequence who he is or what he was doing here. Suffice to say, I simply wanted to check that you were feeling better and to assure you I, too, have fears, but I don't let them put me to the floor and entice me to crawl under my desk."

That was a low blow. It wasn't as if she'd enjoyed being a fool in front of a complete stranger. He'd obviously relayed her frightened scramble. Probably thought it was funny. She stiffened her spine and lifted her chin. Two could play this game. "Is there anything else I can help you with? Otherwise, I have things to do." More important pursuits than being chided for a fear she had battled all her life. Coupled with her abandonment issue both emotions sometimes overrode her common sense.

"No, that will be all. Let's hope we are finished with disruptions and storms."

This could be read two ways. Did he mean internal office politics or real life winter storms?

"Yes, I hope so. I can assure you I will try to control my emotions in the future. It's a work in progress." She rose and left the room, pulling the door closed behind her with a soft yet firm click. Silly man. Did he really care about her well-being? A sneaky thought occurred to her. Perhaps he really wanted to know if she knew the name of the man whose handkerchief she had? The tear-damp piece was in her satchel. She'd need to wash and iron it and bring it to work in case she ever saw him again. Someone might know where or who she could return it to. It was a nice lawn kerchief of obvious quality. Whoever he was, he had good taste.

It would have been better if she'd been brought to Mr. Juckland's attention with something great she'd accomplished, instead of being seen cowering in a corner – except he hadn't seen that. It must have been the hug that concerned him, or having a judge's personal assistant fraternizing with a lowly clerk from visiting solicitors?

Yes, probably that.

Back at her desk, her willpower failed and her hand strayed to the side drawer. Among the spare pens, notepads and, paperclips, way at the back lurked a roll of wine gums. She fingered the unopened sweets then withdrew them, tore the tube open and began to steadily chew her way through the total number. Such a bad habit. She'd been a bit tubby when growing up and her mother—her adopted mother—had repeatedly said it wasn't anything to do with her diet. She must have had a fat birth mother. Hardly a nice thing to say to a child, to infer that not only had her birth mother given her away, she'd also been fat. There were some things she missed about him, but her mother's acid comments weren't one of them. The image of her father, his smile, the aroma of tobacco on his clothing as he hugged her, and his soft Scottish brogue as he read stories to her, threatened to return tears to her eyes.

Enough of maudlin thoughts. She screwed up the sweets wrapping, dropped it into the bin for the cleaners to comment on, and brought up an empty document to type the Judge's dictated jury notes in. As she slipped the earphones on she accepted with a sinking stomach that she'd have to get up early in the morning and run the three-mile route around the riverbank trail before leaving for work, just to run off her lack of willpower. And she'd been doing so well with her no-sugar diet until today.

An email pinged. She didn't recognize the sender. The message had to be work-related. None of her friends had this email address. A quick glance at her watch and she closed the small window. She had barely an hour to type the jury notes and send them to the Judge. His work took priority. Today's scenario of thunder, her escape from the boardroom and Mr. Juckland's curiosity had eaten into her time. The message could wait until the morning.

Chapter Two

Antonia leaned against the park bench, hunched, gulping deep breaths and hoping the orange juice and the apple she'd had before leaving her flat didn't make a return appearance. Not a good look to be heading down in a waste paper bin, even if it was only six thirty in the morning and hardly anyone was about. Perhaps she was overdoing this fitness kick? She'd walk the rest of the way back then jump in the shower and dress, ready to catch the seven-thirty train into the city. If she lost her small breakfast would she be able to eat another? Neither of her friends dieted. They laughed at her concern and lack of self-image. Constantly lying to her and telling her red hair and freckles were enchanting and delightful.

Katrina caught up to her as she climbed the stairs to their flat.

"Out busting your boiler again were you darling?" Katrina's Irish lilt took the sting out of her comment.

"Just a three-mile jog, running off yesterday's willpower failed."

"Oh, those wine gums got you again, did they?" She stepped in front and unlocked the door. "Don't you think three flights of stairs twice a day is enough exercise? If you don't mind me saying, it's not making you look any fitter. You look pale this morning, a bit like I must look after my night shift."

This was a gross exaggeration. Katrina never looked ill, even after a stint of ten nights working at the hospital. Her dark black hair fell in a cascade and curled around her neck. With her Irish accent and warm brown eyes men were drawn to her. Antonia had seen the longing in their eyes, but Katrina seemed oblivious to her charms. Now if you were sick, that was different. The nursing instinct was strong in this woman. The first man to discover this would be the one to catch her.

"Do you want the shower first?" Antonia indicated the bathroom door.

"No thanks. I'll just have a wee sit down and unwind. Once you two have left I'll go to bed. Only one more night to go and I'll have four days off."

Jackie wandered out of her room, stretching her long arms above her head, then quickly covered an escaping yawn with one hand. "Morning all." She looked at Antonia and raised her eyebrows. "Do I see running shoes and Lycra? At this hour?" She shook her head and opened the fridge to peer inside. "Anything in here that's interesting for breakfast or do I have to eat fruit and cereal again." Antonia envied how Jackie could consume bacon, eggs, and even sausages with piles of toast and still remain as slim as a lamppost. Leaving her flatmates to sort out their breakfast options and relieved she still had her fruit juice and apple on-board she headed into the bathroom.

They'd met when all three were flat hunting without success. Sitting in the rental agent's office filling out forms they'd struck up a conversation about the cost of deposits, references required and the hefty price of accommodation. By the time the agent was free to see one of them the three girls had decided to pool their resources and rent together. This meant they could afford a three-bedroom flat in a nice district. The arrangement worked well.

Back at her desk the unopened email winked at her from a sidebar. No doubt more work from one of the judges out on circuit. She opened it and read the contents. Her brow creased and she read it again.

'Could we meet for lunch tomorrow, Saturday, at the Brown Goose, Victoria Street, at noon? I predict a fine day, blustery winds, occasional showers but no thunderstorms. Please bring my handkerchief. Cheers from the man in the cupboard.'

Antonia wasn't sure if she should be delighted with the

lunch invitation, or offended that he demanded his handkerchief back so soon. She hadn't had time to wash it. Was she doing anything tomorrow? In all honesty, no. It was her turn to clean the floors and dust the apartment, but that could be split between Saturday and Sunday. It would be nice to casually say she had a lunch date and waltz off to the center of town. Even if he didn't turn up, she could people watch. His name remained unknown and it hadn't actually been a cupboard, but a small room they had been in. Would she recognize him? Yes, that slightly crooked nose would be a giveaway. Plus, who on earth wore tartan socks with classy jeans? If his dress style remained the same, then it would be a confirmation she had the right man. If two men with slightly bent noses turned up, she'd check their socks. He'd been a little bit handsome and very kind. Lunch might be fun.

Perhaps she could buy him lunch? Some men were a bit touchy about girls being independent. She'd sound him out when the bill came. If he turned up. Then there was the matter of him telling Mr Juckland about her crawling along the floor of the boardroom. Having him buy her lunch would mitigate the embarrassment he'd caused. Weighing all these thoughts, temptation won.

She hit reply and noted the email had been sent from andrew@fisherandfulton. Definitely a firm of solicitors. She'd heard of them. They occupied several floors of one of the inner city buildings. She typed: 'Thank you, will be there, Antonia Prebble' and hit the send key before she could change her mind.

So his name was Andrew, unless someone called Andrew had sent it on his behalf. Why else would he have signed it as 'the man from the cupboard'. Perhaps he was trying to be funny. It really didn't matter. A lunch date didn't pop into her inbox every day of the week. She reached into her desk drawer and relief tinged a flash of disappointment.

Thank heavens she hadn't replaced the wine gums. In moments of stress she ate the damn things by the handful. Perhaps she'd have to swop to jellied alligators. Might be less fattening.

The Brown Goose was more upmarket than its name might imply, definitely not a pub. More of a classy restaurant and as she browsed a copy of the menu from the comfort of a leather chair in the foyer she watched several men enter. None of them looked Andrew-like in the very latest fashion of torn jeans with frayed rips about the knees and thighs. He might have worn jeans, but, if she remembered correctly, at no time had she spotted any flesh through frayed tears in the cloth. Just to be sure she checked each nose and then their socks. While doing this a pair of tan loafers with tassels walked into her view. A muted tartan sock adorned each foot and as she raised her gaze upward over smart dress Chinos and past a chambray denim shirt there he stood. The slightly crooked nose and a thatch of deep brown hair that matched his eyes confirmed his presence. Andrew Whoever had arrived for lunch.

She felt a tide of heat rise from her breast. Just what she didn't need, a red face to match her hair. He dropped into the chair beside her with an air of ownership and smiled.

"Sorry I'm a bit late. Traffic and parking. Becoming more of a hassle each time I come into town." His brow creased. "What about you? Any trouble parking?"

"None at all, I caught the train. I don't use a car in the city." If he'd been fishing to find out what wheels she drove he now knew she didn't. She dropped the menu onto the glass-topped table between them.

He nodded. "Right. Good idea. I should've done the same." He stood and offered his hand to help her out of the chair. She hadn't run another three kilometers this morning to be helped out of a chair, even if she had almost disappeared into the folds of leather. She stood as quickly as she could with a quiet "thank you, I'm fine." This didn't stop him from holding her elbow in a light grasp and guiding her into the restaurant past the Maitre D' who gave him a slight nod. Andrew steered her to a seat by the window, pulled out a chair and waited for her to be seated before he sat opposite her across the starched white linen tablecloth. Despite the tango, which a dozen butterflies are now dancing in her chest, she decided to take the initiative, but as she opened her mouth to ask him his name he began to talk.

"Thank you so much for coming today. Bit of a cheek really as you don't even know my name. I apologize. I'd thought we might have exchanged emails for a few days and become better acquainted, but your brief reply rather stalled that idea. I thought I might have piqued your curiosity."

"I've been frantically busy. I'm the P.A. to one of the Judges and he's a bit of a tyrant if the work isn't ready on time." She forced a smile to mitigate her lapse. "I apologize for my short reply."

"Not at all, it's me who should be apologizing. I've heard that Juckland called you into his office. I hope he didn't embarrass you."

Well, he had, but she couldn't really say so. They hadn't even eaten yet and she was determined to have that embarrassing memory glossed over by a good meal. "It wasn't pleasant. He made a comment about me crawling around the floor. It would've been better if you hadn't mentioned that."

He picked up his serviette and flicked it open. "Sorry, I was trying to explain how frightened you were. I didn't mean to embarrass you." The serviette disappeared between the table and his waist. "Juckland can be a bit of a pompous ass at times."

She couldn't reply to that comment, tempting as it was. Who knew which way gossip traveled between offices and how often, but it obviously did get exchanged. Again, she went to speak, but he beat her to it.

"I guess I gave away a bit too much information trying to explain my own actions."

He smiled and at that moment she could have forgiven him anything at all but needed to bring this conversational thread to a halt.

"Can we just forget about it?"

He nodded.

"Do you think you could tell me your name? You know mine, and I don't even know who you are."

He grinned and his eyes twinkled. "But of course, Miss Prebble." He stood and stepped to her side and reached for her hand. "I'm Andy Mason. I'm pleased to meet you." He shook it firmly and raised his eyebrows, the model of formality. "And you are?"

'You know who I am."

"I do, but only second hand. You haven't introduced yourself."

Getting into the swing of this game he wanted to play she answered, "Antonia Prebble at your service, Mr Mason." He still held her hand and with a gentle tug she removed it and tucked a stray hair behind her ear. "Some of my friends call me Toni."

"May I?"

"Are you my friend or is this a business luncheon?"

He shrugged. "It's an apology luncheon after which we might end up as friends. Agreed?" She nodded. "Good, now let's see what's on the menu today. Order whatever you please, I'm paying, so you can have caviar if you want to."

She'd tried it once and didn't like the fishy taste but there were other delicious things on the menu, especially the desserts. Swallowing the butterfly wings fluttering in her throat, she took a quiet, slow breath and concentrated on the offerings listed. How stupid to be this flustered over a simple lunch but her gaze flitted up and down the page. Her taste buds chose and then discarded each course until the temptation of scallops as an entree followed by lobster as the main won the day, but there'd be no room for dessert. She mentally discarded the entree. Lobster followed by Banoffee, grilled banana coated with caramel toffee and ice-cream – sounded delish. She laid the menu down and looked through the window at the river. Willows hung low, their fronds dangling into the deep green flow. Ripples caught the watery sunlight and behind the trees a dark cloud moved menacingly to block the sun. A brace of ducks scooted out from under the bank in a rush, their wings belting the water as they lifted, honking and squawking into the sky. Behind them on the bank a large black cat stood stiff-legged, its tail thrashing. A missed opportunity by the look of the cat's body language. Taking on a duck for dinner seemed a bit ambitious. Obviously a cat with attitude. That's what she needed – attitude and a bit more self-confidence and this could be her opportunity to begin practicing. Andrew still hadn't told her what he did. She'd winkle that out of him over lunch.

He couldn't believe her casual attitude toward him. Women often simpered, fluttered their eyelashes and giggled when in his company. Antonia's calm air delighted him. But then she didn't really know who he was. Obviously, Juckland, for all his faults and arrogance, had kept Andrew's surname and position to himself. And the longer he could keep this attractive redhead oblivious to his wealth and position the better. He'd had his fill of fortune hunters.

"Are you ready to order?"

"I am. I'll have the lobster for mains, followed by the Banoffee for dessert, thank you."

No hesitation there. If anything annoyed him more than someone who talked constantly about banal activities, it was someone who ordered and then didn't eat their meal. "Good decision." He raised his finger and a waiter appeared at his elbow, pad at the ready. "Would you like a glass of wine?" She hesitated, seeming to consider.

"Why not? I don't have to drive the train. One glass should leave me capable of walking steadily." Her smile, wide and warm, wrinkled around her eyes.

"Any preference?"

"Goodness no. Just something light and white will be great. I know white wine goes with fish and red with beef, but that's the extent of my knowledge. You choose."

What totally refreshing honesty. He ordered a local well-known brand, not too expensive or pretentious, in keeping with the image he wanted to project today.

"So what exactly do you do at Fisher and Fulton?" Her hazel eyes pinned him under her raised eyebrows, twin auburn arches on pale skin. No sunbed tan on this lady. A sprinkling of tiny freckles dressed the bridge of her nose and trailed across her cheeks like a dusting of sand. He had his answer ready. He'd been prepared for this, but he hadn't expected to find her so attractive.

"Andrew?"

"Sorry, daydreaming." He shook his head. "What do I do?" He paused, sucked in his cheeks and proceeded to lie his head off. "I'm learning the ropes really." Not quite true. He knew all the ropes but was always looking for rope-tricks that his employees might be performing. "And although I have a degree I'm fairly low down the totem pole." He did have a degree, but not in law and he actually sat at the top of the totem pole.

"Are you hoping to make partner status eventually?"

Another sensible question followed by another lie. "Yes, that would be a goal to aim for but it might take a few years. I'd need to be invited to the position." No one would invite him to be a partner. He appointed the partners, owned the firm and several other law firms and businesses.

"What field do you specialize in?"

Was she really interested or being polite?

"I started in Conveyancing." Perfectly true, but years ago. "But I'm now deeply involved in acquisitions and due diligence." At last a truthful statement and he was able to relax, his conscience salved a little by one honest truth. Good to know he still had a conscience. He'd intended to enjoy today's lunch and to charm Miss Prebble with a host of untruths, yet now it seemed a stupid idea. Her naivety disarmed him. She appeared to him like a sunflower, shining bright and gold, lighting up the restaurant on a blustery autumn day. "What about you? Any wild ambitions?" Anything to turn the conversation away from him.

"I don't know about 'wild'. More like hopeful intentions." She smiled ruefully, twisting her serviette as if it were threatening to escape. "I'd like to become a legal executive. Being Judge Harding's P.A. is demanding, but not very satisfying. Typing jury notes and court reports can be depressing. It's all evidence of the worst side of life and I'd like to move into more of an administrative role within a law firm." Again her gaze captured his heart. "So if you hear of any positions going at Fisher and Fulton could you let me know? I'm tired of typing depressing reports about the dreadful things people do to each other."

"What sort of things?"

"You know I can't repeat anything from the court's files. Just like you wouldn't tell me any details of your latest negotiations or discoveries made during due diligence. Would you?"

"You're quite right. I wouldn't. I shouldn't have asked."

Not only honest, but ethical as well. He'd love to employ her tomorrow, but that would then reveal his true position and because he started this lie it now trapped him. "I'll keep you in mind, not that anyone ever tells me about future vacancies." Absolutely true. Well out of his sphere of interest. Someone else hired and fired the staff. Just inquiring would trigger alarm bells with his managers.

Their meals arrived and they ate in silence until Antonia finished and after placing her cutlery together and wiping her mouth she continued. "But surely you must hear office gossip. Some of your female staff must take maternity leave or join other firms."

Regret swamped him. What had he got himself into? "I feel like someone from Human Resources being expected to find work for a lunch companion." His joke fell flat.

Her face stiffened, her back straightened. "My apologies," she said. "I presumed we were dining as friends. Obviously this is a business luncheon and I've over-stepped the mark. Forget I even mentioned it." She turned and looked out the window, effectively ignoring him.

Now he'd upset her. He wasn't used to being cut down so quickly.

"I didn't really mean that. It was a comment in bad taste. Of course, this is a friendly luncheon. Let's not talk business at all." Would this mollify her?

She met his gaze once more. "Very well. Tell me something about yourself. Why have you made a study of the weather?"

What had made her ask this? He creased his brow, trying to remember what would have triggered her question.

When he didn't answer she continued, "You said during our brief meeting in the stationery closet that the thunderstorm would pass and you knew this because you made a study of the weather."

A sliver of personal information that now returned to

haunt him. "I sail…yachts of various sizes."

"Harbor or ocean going?"

"I've crewed occasionally on ocean races." No need to say he'd owned the boat. "You have to be able to read weather maps and the sky. It's not nice to be caught in sudden squalls." She nodded. "What about you? Any hobbies?"

"I run. Sometimes I walk. I'd like to get fit enough to do a half marathon in the future, but that's a wild dream, totally unobtainable if I'm being honest."

"And are you always honest?" The notion amused him.

"Yes, I try to be. Don't you?"

Their dessert arrived and saved him from answering.

The gentle rocking of the train lulled her and mixed with the two glasses of wine she'd had with lunch, she almost missed her station. Walking home, she pondered their conversation. The feeling that Andrew hadn't been very open about himself continued to niggle her. In the end, she'd tired of him deflecting her questions and it seemed he'd run out of things to ask her. After all, growing up in a small town wasn't an exciting history. He already knew where she worked and what she did, which only left basic things like did she have a significant 'other', and whether she had any siblings. No, to both of those questions. What had she learned about him? Very little. Just a lot of bluff and bluster and talk of wine, food and some of the places overseas he'd found interesting. But why he went overseas and what he did while he was there, were never answered either.

On the way up the stairs she met Katrina coming down on her way to her afternoon shift. Katrina paused. "How was your date?"

"More of an apology luncheon, definitely not a date."

"Are you going to see him again?"

"I doubt it, but I've been wined and dined at an expensive restaurant so that's a pretty good apology. Now I'm about to start on the weekend cleaning so you won't be woken by a vacuum cleaner in the morning. You can sleep in."

"That'll be sheer bliss," and they parted ways, one up, one down.

Inside the flat Jackie lay sprawled on the couch, her face covered in slices of cucumber. "Can't sit up, darling, I'm improving my complexion." This remark from a girl with faultless skin. Perhaps cucumbers did work.

"Not a problem, you just lie there because I'm about to attack the flat."

"How did your date go?" One of the cucumber slices moved and Jackie poked it back into place.

"The luncheon was great," Antonia said, "and the company was attractive but he seemed distracted and a bit vague. I've come home feeling as if I were an obligation he needed to fulfill." She tossed her bag onto her bed, changed into a pair of slacks and began her cleaning stint. It seemed an appropriate punishment for thinking she might have been asked out because he had found her attractive and wanted to see her again. She might just hang on to that handkerchief, because he hadn't asked for it and she'd forgotten to give it to him.

Chapter Three

The following two weeks passed in repetition with court documents and reports to be transcribed; plus she sorted out the Judge's forthcoming travel arrangements around the circuit. Antonia shook her head in wonder when an email from Andrew arrived in her inbox.

'Would you like to go sailing on Saturday? The weather forecast promises gentle breezes, no thunderstorms lurking. I have the use of a small yacht. Cheers, Andrew'

She ignored the frisson of delight that swirled in her stomach and tried to consider the offer as she would any other offer of entertainment. Did she have anything else on? Only a weekend of running, walking and wearing out her feet followed by evenings watching the Outlander series on Netflix. A chance to go sailing would be different and something she'd never done before. She had lots of warm clothes from her exercise regime so could fit herself out in a warm jacket and trainers. Yes, she'd go, but she would hesitate, as a lady should, before she replied.

The next day a further email arrived.

'Do you want to come? Please let me know ASAP. Need to book the yacht.'

So he wasn't going with a crowd and truly did want her company. She quickly hit reply and typed 'Yes please. What time and where?' Then hit send before she could change her mind. She would check in with Aunty Google over the next few days and learn what she could about sailing. Shouldn't be too hard. The America's Cup had been on the sports channel recently. There was nothing more nautical than that.

Saturday morning found her on the Salisbury Jetty. She'd arrived a bit early because that's how the train schedule worked and she hadn't wanted to be late. He might think she'd stood him up. She checked her phone. Nearly half nine and no sign of a white sail approaching.

They had exchanged mobile numbers and she'd offered to bring a picnic. It presently sat at her feet in a plastic box at the bottom of a large cloth bag; along with warmer clothes in case she got wet. The water reflected the landscape in a mirror image, broken occasionally by small waves as it stretched into the distance up the harbor behind the island that protected it from the sea. The distance ranges smudged the horizon, a thin line of snow on their crest and the only clouds visibly lined up above them as if waiting to roll down the hills and dowse the land below. A breeze wrapped several strands of hair across her face and she took her cap from the bag, put it on and pulled her hair through the gap at the back. She'd tied the Auburn mess into a ponytail earlier knowing it would be a nuisance in the wind. At least she didn't have to impress the man. That chance had gone. All she had to do was enjoy the day.

"Antonia."

She turned and there he was, the boat bobbing beside the jetty, a small motor puttering at the stern. Wasn't that cheating, using a motor?

"I was looking for a boat with a sail up."

"I'll do that later. You need to get on board first. Can you manage?" He tossed a rope around the bollard above him and tied it to something on the deck. Obviously this held the craft against the steps, but it still rocked.

The bag was a little heavier than she intended so she maneuvered down the steps sideways, propping the bag on the step above each time, and then stopped before the bottom. The last two planks above the waterline were covered in slime. The water rose and fell as if it couldn't make up its mind whether to flood the next step or remain where it was. The side of the boat wouldn't keep still either.

Could she risk a large step between waves? She didn't know. And what about the bag and their lunch?

A strong hug lifted her off the steps and plonked her into the small craft and a moment later the bag landed beside her feet. She slid to one side, searching behind with her hands to find the seat, and then tucked the bag into a corner of the cabin.

"Sorry, I sort of froze."

"I noticed." But Andrew's grin removed any criticism of her lack of action. "Sit tight, we're off." He flicked the rope off the bollard, sat at the tiller and the motor sputtered into life. "I'll get us out of the traffic before I put the sail up."

Once through a bevy of small boats, he passed her a lifejacket and she put it on under his instructions. "Can't have you going overboard," he declared, "Judge Harding would probably lock me up."

The wharf drifted away from them. No, it was them moving, not the wharf. The motor cut and the slap-slap of the waves on the side of the boat became the loudest sound. A seagull screamed and dived across the bow to land on the water, then lifted with a piece of food in its beak. Another gull on a stealing mission joined it in flight. Andrew clambered onto the cabin roof and hauled the ropes to raise the mainsail. Once that was up, he pulled other ropes to rig the small sail in the front.

"Here, hold this." He handed her a rope end. "You can help."

"But I don't know how to sail."

He shook his head. "Hold it anyway. It'll make you feel as if you're in control."

And it did. Suddenly the song in the rigging wires and the breeze in her face filled her with a sense of exhilaration. No noisy motors, just nature moving them along. Andrew moved back to the tiller. Strong ropes ran through eyelets on the side and he held them, grouped in his fingers, playing them constantly. She followed his gaze to the small colored strings anchored near the top of the mast. She forgot their name but she knew from her research that these floating ribbons told him when the boat was trimmed correctly.

"I'm going to take us up the harbor to an inlet on the island. We have to cross the harbor mouth and it will be a bit rough. The incoming tide is fighting with the water going out. The boat will tilt as the wind shifts. I'll have to tack and it'll be choppy. Try not to scream."

An order not a suggestion. The cheek of the man. She wouldn't scream now even if she got tipped out. "I've read about tacking. Will I have to duck?"

"Probably not, but you might like to swap to the lower side to be more comfortable."

She nodded and held onto the rope he'd given her until she realized her fingers were cramping. She released her grip a little and the yacht continued to sail its course. As predicted the waves at entrance tossed the craft about even though they were a good distance within the harbor. A line of white surf sat on the horizon where the harbor met the sea. Despite the balmy weather the power of the current awed her. She could feel the swoop of the wind as it caressed the water. The chilly breeze made her ears ache. Any conversation had to be conducted in shouts and she gave up trying. She wished she'd packed a beanie to pull down over her ears. The breeze had an edge to it as if the mountains further south had their first dusting of snow.

An hour later he turned the yacht toward a sandy beach. "I'm going to run her up on the sand, but I need to lift the centerboard. Can you come here and hold the tiller firm?"

"What about my rope?" She raised it a little.

"Just drop it on the floor."

Had she heard him right? "Really? What will happen?"

"Absolutely nothing. It's not connected to anything. It was to make you feel better."

She momentarily felt affronted then saw the sense of it and laughed. As she exchanged places with him she thumped him on the arm. "That was a wicked thing to do."

"But it worked. Didn't it?" For the first time, she saw a man totally relaxed and in his element. His hair, now sticky with salt, stood on end. His grin traveled to his eyes and now laughed with her, not at her. He seemed exceedingly attractive and her heart rate increased. She turned her face into the wind to cool her skin, knowing a blush had risen in response to her thoughts. He didn't appear to notice.

The boat juddered, slid and stopped. Andrew jumped into the shallow water and carried the anchor up to the beach and dug it in the sand. He returned to guide her over the cabin roof to the bow and lifted her onto the sand.

"Lunch?" She pointed to the deck where she'd retrieved the bag and propped it among the ropes and wires. He climbed back on board and disappeared into the cabin. Moments later he rejoined her, a rug over his arm, a bottle of wine in one hand and the lunch bag in his shoulder. They retreated to the base of a bank, fortunately angled so that the wind skimmed over their heads. In the lee of the grass-topped mound they leaned back on the roots of the two huge Pohutukawa trees that stood above them. With the sand molded into comfortable hollows beneath them, they spread the food out on the blanket. Above her the leaves of the evergreen pohutakawas rustled and whispered their secrets. Several gulls swooped and settled in the high branches in expectation of sharing their meal. Despite the chill a sense of warm happiness infused her. She leaned against the tree roots and gazed southward toward home. A day like this made her glad she'd moved to the city.

She wouldn't push a conversation today. If he wanted to talk - well and good. If he chose to remain silent, then she would, too. A companionable silence surrounded their meal. Without tension or conversation they shared the food and wine, exchanging smiles of appreciation. Dusting the crumbs from her jacket and wiping her mouth, she began to gather up the containers and disposable plates, waiting for him to start a conversation. His initial subject rather surprised her.

"I buried a good friend near here." Out of the blue, no lead-up, just 'he'd buried a friend nearby'.

"But there isn't a graveyard. Is there?" She looked around, puzzled. No headstones, no fenced in area, just sand and grassed banks on each side of their picnic spot. "Did you get permission?"

"No, I didn't ask. I just brought him here and dug a hole, just over there," he pointed to a small rise, "where there's a good view of the ranges. He loved hunting wild pigs in the bush."

A suspicion rose and she ran with it. This man seemed to converse obliquely. "Did your friend have four legs?"

"He did." He pulled his gaze from the hills and looked at her. "You're very perceptive. How did you know?"

Were those tears in his eyes, or the wind making them water?

"I've had dogs myself and it's what I would've done, if I'd had a boat and could sail." She didn't say the sadness in his eyes gave him away. "Besides burying a friend at the bottom of the garden is a bit mundane after years of faithful friendship. Been there, done that." She remembered her childhood. "Everyone needs a friend who never judges, never criticizes, who doesn't care who you are or what you do - just loves."

She watched as he searched for a handkerchief and pulled a crisp white model from his pocket. She still hadn't returned the one he'd lent her. It sat folded and ironed on her bedside table waiting for her to remember. Perhaps subconsciously she didn't want to give it back. She turned her head away to give him the privacy of wiping his eyes and blowing his nose. So he had a soft center after all. Now she had another fact to add to the small pile she was collecting – he'd once owned a dog.

"And one other thing, Andrew. You seem to be fairly law-abiding. I can't picture you carrying a dead friend over your shoulder, digging a six-foot-long hole and burying him illegally – unless you killed him; and that would be murder. I don't think you're capable of that."

A cloud passed over his face, dulling his eyes and wiping the sunshine from his face. "Don't you believe it. I easily could be, if provoked." His answer had a chill to it. The set of his jaw and how he now turned his back, annoyed her. How childish. It had been a throwaway remark.

She stood up. The wine had loosened her tongue too much. "Now I've upset you. I'm sorry. Let's clear up and go home." She'd spoiled the day simply by making a joke, though murder was no joke at the best of times. She knew so little about this man she should have been more careful with smart remarks. But if he'd been more open perhaps she wouldn't have said it. Too late now. "It's a lovely spot to buy a friend," she murmured in apology.

The return trip seemed faster; downwind and with a small spinnaker up the yacht flew over the wave tops. At the jetty he helped her up the steps and stood rather awkwardly, looking around, looking anywhere, everywhere, but at her. She knew that feeling: the frozen stance, the hurt in his eyes. What memory had her murder remark triggered? She hated invisible walls of defense. They shouted pain and explained nothing.

"Thank you Andrew, for the lovely day. It was superb. I will never forget it." She broke through his wall and stepped into his personal space, as her father did to her when she threw a wall up. She wrapped her arms around him and he stiffened, then his muscles gave under her hands and his spine softened.

"Yes, it was great." He nodded several times. "Could we do it again... sometime?"

The hesitation before 'sometimes' offended her. She stepped back. "I don't think so. I have holidays due and I might go home for a while." Who needed such a touchy friend? He was hard work. It took all the enjoyment out of the day. "The judge is away on circuit for two months." The idea rolled out as it occurred to her. She could work from the District Court at home. She could work from anywhere while Judge Harding traveled. "I'll do the Judge's work from the local courthouse at home."

"So you won't be in the city?"

She swore a flash of disappointment crossed his face, but then she could have imagined it. "No, not for a while." She picked up her bag, considerably lighter than it had been this morning and slipped it over her shoulder. "Bye, Andrew, and thank you again." Without a backward glance she strode off toward the rail station. Men! Who needed them? She wasn't going to stand there while he walked away and abandoned her and their nebulous friendship.

"Where's home?"

Was that Andrew's voice? Or had the wind snatched that query from someone else? She didn't turn back. He'd had hours to find out where her home was and he'd never once asked. Self-centered and touchy, she could add those two facts to the small pile of knowledge she had on Andrew Mason. At least she wouldn't be tempted to contact him because, despite several queries that he'd deflected without answering, she didn't know where he lived. Two sort-of dates and so little information exchanged. Not a good foundation to build a friendship on. An ill-fated friendship; but she had been up the harbor on a yacht – across the wide entrance, tossed and flicked by the current—plus a picnic and a bottle of wine. Quite a good haul of experiences even if it all came to a stop today.

This time, she walked away first, and wasn't left somewhere to be chosen by strangers.

Chapter Four

On the following Monday morning Antonia discussed her decision with the Judge. By Tuesday, he agreed she could work from the district court offices while he was on circuit. On Wednesday morning Mr Juckland popped into her office and said he'd actioned Judge Harding's instructions. An office at Hampton Downs had been arranged for her with access to the Court admin system. Late Thursday evening she rang her mother to say she was coming home for a few weeks. Done and dusted. As long as she paid her share of the rent Katrina and Jackie promised not to let her room. She could spend time with her ill father and still be gainfully employed. A holiday of sorts, a break from the city. Was she running away? She told herself she wasn't.

On Friday morning, Mr. Juckland asked her if she'd like to carry some hard copy files to Fisher and Fulton regarding a misrepresentation case the crown prosecutors were working on. He could have used a courier, but said he preferred to trust confidential files to his staff. She agreed. With Judge Harding en route to the most distant court of his circuit, she effectively had nothing to do. The files were in a carry-along trundler and with the wind whipping the leaves off the trees, she strolled the five blocks into the main street.

In a fit of pique and curiosity, she asked the receptionist at the main desk if Andrew Mason were in, only to be greeted with a blank stare and a slow shake of her head. 'Never heard of him,' was the comment. Not surprising if he was low on the totem pole. On her way to the top floor, she sneaked glances around to see if she could find where he might be, a conveyance lawyer tucked away in a side office perhaps? The idea of a quick 'Hiya' wave at his doorway and an equally quick departure rather appealed to her.

A personal assistant on the third floor directed her toward the boardroom where the merger files were secured and in the passageway, lined with photographs of the past and present board members, she paused to study the old fogies that ran this well-known business.

And there he was, dressed in smart finery! A perfectly fitting suit, posh tie, slicked back hair – only his name was different: 'Andrew M. Maletto, Chairman of Board of Directors'.

What a liar the man was. Rage rose and flooded her face. Just as well no one could see. She clenched her fists and cursed quietly. Not only was he arrogant, self-centered and touchy, but a first-class liar as well. Common sense slowly won the day and she calmed. If she hadn't come today she'd never have known how stupid she'd been. He'd fooled her completely. Probably enjoyed every minute of his deception and laughed himself silly over her innocent queries and her interest in his life. What a fool she'd been. Better to find out now. Any future emails arriving in her inbox from andrew@fisherandfulton would be promptly deleted – unread. She might be easily fooled twice, but not three times. She handed the files over the security clerk and signed them into his custody, then in case Andrew lurked in the building, she took the lift to the basement carpark, walked the stairs up to street level and strode back to her office. Mr Juckland's query as to whether the files arrived safely was answered with a curt snap. Did he know they'd been sailing? Was he part of the deception? More likely he sent her over there, tempting fate that she would meet Andrew again because to Mr Juckland's knowledge she had no idea who had comforted her in the stationery closet. Just as well she was going to work from the district office. She needed time for her anger to fade and to become objective about Andrew M. Maletto.

_____//_____

Andrew looked out of the sixth-floor windows over the cityscape. He'd been stonewalled at every turn when he'd tried to find Antonia's hometown. Frustration drove him as he paced his office. He'd be better off going for a run. He flopped in his large leather chair, his hands clasped behind his head. A headache lurked behind his brow threatening to move to his eyes and down his neck. He wasn't used to being stonewalled, but today the Privacy Act had been quoted to him at every turn. Power had become a bandage to his damaged emotions and today the bandage threatened to lift; feeling cross threatened to become a surge of anger. He took several deep breaths and reconsidered his options.

It seemed you could no longer just ring up and ask where someone was spending their holiday, nor would a personal contact number be given to you, unless instructions had been left for it to be released. Searching for another avenue of information he wondered if Antonia voted? He turned to his computer and searched the Electoral Roll. It showed an address for an Antonia Prebble in the suburb of Highcliffe. He remembered she'd mentioned sharing an apartment. Perhaps he could go there and see if he could sweet-talk her flatmates into revealing her hometown. Once he had the location he'd be able to track her down through the court's offices.

Mr Juckland had seemed amused by his inquiries and Andrew suspected Juckland had quite enjoyed saying 'no he couldn't possibly reveal such personal information.' Only when Andrew said he and Antonia had lunched and been sailing did Juckland raise his eyebrows, smirk and deign to answer.

"Really? She never mentioned it to me." Sounding doubtful, he added, "Miss Prebble is working from a district court while Judge Harding travels the circuit. The Judge will be away for a month and Miss Prebble indicated she will be away from her office for the whole time." Then he'd tilted his chin and looked down his rather short, fat nose, adding, "I'm sure if Miss Prebble wanted you to know where she was going to be she would have told you during the two outings you say you shared with her."

Andrew rubbed his head, remembering how he wanted to dismiss the man, but Mr Juckland wasn't one of his employees. Again the Privacy Act was muttered about as a final comment and Andrew had delivered a polite and unwarranted 'thank you' and resisted the urge to slam the door on his way out of Juckland's office.

His conscience told him it was his own fault. Used to having employees jump to his every wish and command, he now suffered in a position of weakness. The Privacy Act ruled supreme. Bigger problems than this hadn't defeated him. Surely he could find her himself. He'd crawled his way to the top with a good dose of determination, coupled with a hefty inheritance. He'd rather not have had the inheritance— and still had his parents.

He thought he'd overcome that trauma, but perhaps he hadn't? Did the wall he'd built to protect his feelings prevent him from being a decent person? And why, if he'd found Antonia so attractive, had he failed to ask those personal questions? 'Fool', his conscience chided. 'Too busy lying'.

He relived the picnic, trying to pinpoint when he'd offended her. What had he said? They'd been talking about him burying his friend...his dog. She'd guessed, which proved how perceptive she was. Then she'd mentioned murder and she didn't think him capable of that—and that, he remembered, was when anger had flooded his brain, a red mist of rage. What had he said? Hours of counseling and still he wanted to kill the drunkard who'd driven into his parents' car and killed them – along with his beloved dog. If he hadn't been so proud and arrogant he could have explained there and then; told her all the personal things he'd only shared with his therapist. But no, his old habit of hiding his emotions had surfaced. He'd clammed up, shut out her voice and sailed the boat back to the wharf in silence, driving the small craft as if it were a bullet. Only as she walked away did he realize he wanted to see her again and how little he knew about her. Had she heard his query? Or did she ignore it?

He searched his memory for facts of her private life. If he didn't have the information then he hadn't asked. Too busy batting away her queries and making up lies, yet she'd only been making conversation. In truth, she gave up her curiosity far quicker than most women did. She only knew of him as Andrew Mason, a lowly lawyer working at Fisher and Fulton. Would knowing his true position have made any difference? He may never know, unless he could track her down.

In the week following their harbor trip he'd sent an email asking if they could go sailing again; followed three days later querying whether she'd received the email and repeating his request. The second week he'd suggested she might like to go to a show. There were visiting Irish singers at the local theatre, or he could get tickets to the National Symphony's performance the weekend after? Still no reply. By the third week he'd added to his emails the attachment that the sender wished to be notified if the email was read. It appeared his emails were not opened but they must have been received because none had bounced back. He had his secretary ring and the Judges' chambers confirmed Ms Prebble was 'out of the office.'

Today, now the beginning of the fourth week, he had resorted to a personal search. Confronting Juckland in his lair had only resulted in the other man looking sanctimoniously superior and quoting the Privacy Act. He glanced at the time. If he left now he could reach the address in Highcliffe and sit in his car and wait for someone to enter the address. He shrugged away the thought it could be construed as stalking. Nonsense, men of his stature didn't stalk—they searched diligently.

_____//_____

The apartment appeared to be above a block of shops. The entrance at street level had the number and B next to the mail slot. He pressed the buzzer on the intercom panel and waited, not really expecting a reply. A woman answered.

"Have you forgotten your key again, Jackie?"

"No, it's Andrew Mason speaking." He took a breath and hurried on. "I'm a friend of Antonia's and I wondered if I could get her present address from you? You're her flatmate, aren't you?"

The pause lengthened until he wondered if the intercom had been disconnected. He turned the collar of his coat up against the wind. Just as he'd given up and was about to turn away the perky voice with an Irish lilt returned, "Oh, you're THAT Andrew Mason, the man who isn't actually Andrew Mason at all. Well, m'darling, I'm not sure Antonia wants to see you again, let alone me giving you her address."

"Please. Could I just talk to you for a few moments?" He hadn't felt this stupid since he'd been a teenager, asking a girl for a date. Standing on the sidewalk, pleading into an intercom system wasn't a good look. Thankfully, no one seemed to care. Pedestrians hurried past or turned into the small convenience store next door.

"You could be an ax murderer for all I know, just pretending to be Andrew Mason."

"But I'm not!" His voice had risen with frustration. Women could be so oblique in their conversation, going off in tangents away from the matter at hand. Why did they take so much convincing?

"Who's pretending to be Andrew Mason?" A voice at his shoulder demanded and he turned to find a tall blond beside him. She reached over and pressed the button. "Hi

Katrina, I'm at the door. Is this man worrying you?"

Perhaps he'd have better luck with this one?

"Do you want to bring him up, Jackie? He's after Antonia's location. I'm not sure if we should give it to him. Does he look reputable, or dangerous? Any axes visible?"

Jackie's gaze traveled down and up. He stood tall and smiled, hoping his sincerity and non-ax-murdering qualities were obvious. He suspected these two women were having fun with his predicament.

"Looks a bit overdressed for Highcliffs but we should be safe. If I knew how, I'd frisk him. I'll bring him up."

She unlocked the door, ushered him through and clicked the lock behind them. The stairs were narrow and well-worn with slight hollows in the middle of the wooden treads. A bare light bulb hung from a long electrical cord halfway up and at the top landing a narrow window allowed in enough light to display the water stain on the cream wall, dressed in a patina of dust.

The interior of the flat couldn't have been more in contrast. White walls, bright rugs and colored throws decorated the space. In one corner a kitchen could be seen, like a long closet and a small dining table sat under the front window. He stood looking down on the street while Jackie disappeared into a room, to change she'd said, and he presumed the Irish lilt would emerge eventually from wherever she'd disappeared to.

"Sorry, I've just woken. I'm Katrina." He turned to meet a compact lady, dark curls, brown eyes and the owner of the Irish accent. "I'm on night shift this week. I didn't think you'd want to see my pajamas." Her smile reached her eyes as he grasped her outreached hand.

"Pleased to meet you. I'm sorry to interrupt your lives, but I'm trying to find Antonia. I know she's away, staying at home while she continues her work for Judge Harding." He could hear himself babbling, but couldn't seem to stop. "No one will tell me where she is and…" What could he say? "I need to see her. I need to apologize. I'd really like to begin our friendship again." He realized he still had Katrina's hand and let it go. She tilted her head and studied him.

"I'd say you certainly need to apologize. Such a load of lies you told that girl. Why would you do that?"

The direct question threw him. People didn't question him like this. "My reasons were personal. I'll explain them to Antonia." He glanced out the window. It had started to rain. "I don't feel I need to explain my motives to you, we've just met." Even to his ears, he sounded as pompous as Mr Juckland.

"But will you apologize and will you tell her the truth? We can't have you hurting her feelings like before." Jackie now stood beside Katrina. "I'm not sure which was the greater, her hurt feelings or her anger at your lies, Mr. Andrew M. Martello."

So she did know. And so did her flatmates, their animosity palpable. He could feel it bouncing off him and swirling around the room. He tried levity to break the impasse.

"If I take you both out for dinner, would that do as an apology? And if you find my company bearable then will you give me her address?" He smiled as his heart cramped and his throat ached. Would they?

"Oh. Bribery and corruption!" Katrina bounced on her toes. "Shall we? I'm not dressed for a slap-up meal, but the local Pizza parlor does a fantastic pepperoni dish. Jackie, what do you think? Are we bribe-able?"

The tall blond twisted her mouth and paused, then smiled and he knew he'd won. "Yes, but no promises mind. You'll need to be very charming before we divulge any information."

It would be a new experience, but good practice, he decided, as, quicker than he'd ever imagined possible the two girls had refreshed their hair and makeup and were leading him down the stairs and onto the street. They hurried along the pavement, hugging close to the buildings to avoid the rain until with high pitched shrieks of 'here we are' 'this way' they dashed into a doorway. He followed them in, trailing along like an afterthought while they chose a table, perused the menu and recommended their favorites. He ordered the food, paid for the drinks and all the time worked harder than he'd done for years to be charming, attentive and above all else interested in their lives and careers.

His reward was an address scribbled on the back of the restaurant's account and a warning they would be telling Antonia he was coming. The rest would be up to her.

"No personal recommendation? No reference to my skill as a charming host?"

But they just smiled and exchanged looks.

"Any advice?" he queried as he tucked the precious slip of paper into his wallet, having memorized the name of the town.

Katrina leaned close and whispered, "Probably best not to tell lies."

Then they hurried off, leaving him alone on the footpath. He walked back to his car and slipped the parking ticket off the windscreen where it had been keeping company with several sodden leaves. He wiped the raindrops off the plastic cover and read the notice: "parking in a resident's parking area without a resident's parking certificate - $60.00" A small price to pay along with dinner to get Antonia's work location if not her home address.

He'd had a great evening. Not once had he been queried about anything more serious than which rugby club he favored to win the national competition and whether he thought a cat would survive in their flat on its own during the day. He'd forgotten how relaxed, normal people could be and the small things that made them happy.

With a surge of hope in his heart he drove home. No use being the boss if you couldn't take time off; tomorrow morning he'd head south in search of Miss Prebble.

Chapter Five

The sunshine highlighted Antonia's father's white hair as he bent over the chess board. He chewed his lip and touched his knight with his good hand, then withdrew it and moved his castle instead. Despite his stroke and his aphasia he could still play chess. Winning made him smile and his pleasure made it worth her time. Sometimes the game continued over two or three nights. His stroke might have robbed him of speech, but his mind remained sharp in places, while blank in others. He'd taught himself to write with his left hand, albeit in wriggly letters and jumbled spelling. With chess, words didn't matter.

Antonia moved her piece and sighed as her father checkmated her. Too distracted to concentrate she raised her hands in defeat and he grunted, almost a laugh but not quite. She needed to talk to him about her quandary. Perhaps talking aloud would solve the dilemma she faced even if he couldn't answer in any great detail.

"Daddy," she began. He leaned closer, tilted his head and raised his eyebrows. "You know Jackie and Katrina, my flatmates?" he nodded, "Well, they've rung to say they've given my work address to the man I went out with a couple of times. I met him through work and he took me out for dinner. We went sailing one day too." Why he'd taken her out for dinner didn't matter at the moment. At least her father couldn't stop her train of thought to ask her that.

Her father spread his hands as if to say 'what's the problem?'

"The thing is, although I liked him a lot and we had a nice time, I found out he'd lied to me about his name and his work. I always had a sneaking feeling he was holding something back." Now her father frowned. "Then the day before I came home, I discovered he was a senior partner and chairman of the board of a large and successful firm of lawyers. They specialize in commercial litigation and arbitration." She looked past her father through the bay window where the winter wind bent the branches of the silver birch, its bare limbs thrashing together. Yes, she'd felt as mad as the tree's branches expressed. She'd wanted to thump something. "He'd told me he was a lowly clerk, hoping to work his way up the corporate ladder." She blinked, feeling her eyes watering. "He was very charming, but sometimes he became surly and even a bit arrogant." She remembered the way he flicked his fingers for a waiter and how the waiter hurried over. "Now I wonder if deep down, he just wanted to be a nobody when we were together. Perhaps that's why he lied about his name." Memories circled as she relived snatches of their conversations. Her father crooked his finger. He wanted her to continue.

"When I found out he'd lied about his name I was hurt and furious. I ranted to the girls about it while I packed to come home. According to Katrina yesterday evening he tracked down where I lived and took the girls out for dinner. He effectively bribed my location out of them." She had to smile at his tactics. "I guess I would have given in as well, he's rather handsome and can be totally charming when he wants to be." She stood and stepped over to the window, peering down the drive. Had he found out where her parents lived yet? That wouldn't be hard now he had the town she lived in. Her father reached back from his chair for her hand and pulled her around, beckoning for more information. "It's not as if I'd forbidden them to tell him. I didn't think he'd even try and find me. The girls said he is full of remorse and seemed genuine. He wants to apologize for being rude and sullen – and telling lies." She sat once more in her chair and clasped her father's left hand. "He'll be turning up sometime soon. He wouldn't have gone to all that trouble not to come, but the thing is Daddy, I don't know if I want to see him. Why be hurt all over again? I thought he liked me and then he didn't. Why lie to someone you like? I felt rejected and you know what that does to me. Now it seems he's still interested." She leaned back and smiled. "I've decided to become a career woman and now he's messing around with my emotions. I've ignored his emails for a month and tried to forget him." She sighed. "I know what will happen when I see him. My heart will flip and I'll want to forgive him." She wound her hair around her fingers. "It's not fair. He has to work to regain my affection." Her father nodded vigorously. "I don't know what to do."

Writing was difficult for her father, yet he reached for his pen and paper and she watched as he wrote.

'LOEV HIM YU DO?'

Did she love him? "Not yet, but I think I could, very easily. He reminds me of an injured puppy and you know I've always been a sucker for animals with broken limbs."

'LSTIEN TO YROU HRTEA,' her father scribbled.

"Yes, I will. I'll see what my heart says when I see him. If it flips and dances I'll give him a second chance. If it doesn't move, then I'll know he's not the one…and I'll stick to my plan to become a legal executive." She raised her father's hand to her lips and kissed it. "Thank you my darling dad. You are so wise." A tear trickled down his face and she leaned forward and brushed it off his cheek with her fingertips. "But…if he tells me one more lie, he's out the door."

With a firm nod, her father agreed.

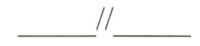

Antonia's fingers flew over the keys. She listened carefully as she typed court orders, decisions and jury notes which piled up in her documents files ready to be printed out and delivered to records. Her phone rang.

"Judge Harding's office," she said.

"Antonia, it's Julie from reception. There's a man here who says he knows you and wants to talk to you. We can't allow him into the court offices. Do you want to speak to him?"

"What's his name?" She could hear a murmur of voices.

"He said his real name is Andrew Mason Maletto, but you know him as Andrew Mason." The receptionist's voice lowered to a whisper. "That sounds a bit dodgy; do you want to speak to him? He looks rather dishy. Nicely dressed and well spoken. Do you know him?"

At least he hadn't lied. "Yes, I'll be down shortly. Could you ask him to wait?"

"Will do."

Julie disconnected and Antonia took several long deep breaths, calmed her inner self, gathered her resolve to be cool calm and collected by remembering his lies. Julie's comment that he was 'rather dishy' reminded her of how handsome and attractive Andrew was. Perhaps now he wasn't pretending to be someone else he might be a nicer person, but first she had to face him and see what he wanted.

She peeked through the one-way glass in the hallway door before she opened it. Yes, her heart stirred a little. Andrew sat in one of a line of straight-backed chairs, flicking through the pages of a dog-eared magazine. Not many people had the desire to sit and read in reception prior to appearing in court. All the magazines had a tired, exhausted look. Nobody thought to replace them. A bit of boredom wouldn't do him any harm. Being bored might be a new experience.

She pushed the door open and entered the room, keeping her expression serious and being as professional as her heart would allow.

"Andrew, nice to see you. What are you doing down this neck of the woods?" No need to say she'd expected him.

He stood, spread his arms, then saw her outstretched

hand and a flash of disappointment crossed his face. Had he seriously thought she would allow him to hug her? In the reception of the Courthouse? Lifting her from the wharf to the boat had been a hug of sorts on his part, and if she remembered correctly, she had been the one to give him a brief hug when they parted. But he would have to work for any more. The hug quota had been reduced severely by his high lie quota.

"Antonia," He gripped her hand. "I've come to apologize for my boorish behavior at the end of our sailing trip. And the fact I lied to you about my surname. I understand you now know my real one?"

She didn't answer. Her jaw ached from keeping her mouth firmly closed.

"I'm truly sorry and I'd like to take you out for a superb meal this evening so we can talk about it. Will you come?"

Another meal in another restaurant? No. She felt something folksier would have to do. He needed to be somewhere out of his comfort zone. "Only if we can go to Chicken in a Bucket, I hear they have great chips."

He nodded. It looked as if he'd agree to a sandwich on the bench outside the court, in a howling gale, if she'd suggested it.

"Can I wait for you after work?"

Julie, at the reception desk, tittered. Antonia reclaimed her hand from his grasp. Although having his hand wrapped around hers kept her heart racing and was rather nice, he'd held it for too long. People were noticing.

"No thank you. I need to go home first and spend some time with my father. I'll meet you there." She looked at her watch. "Say half six?"

"I'm happy to come and collect you."

Heavens, he was persistent. "I have a chess date with my father. He's had a stroke and can't talk, but he's probably plotted out four moves while I've been at work. It may seem a small thing, but it's something I'm doing every day while I'm home. I don't want to disappoint him."

"Of course. I understand." His deep brown eyes showed empathy, his face softened. "Fathers are precious. Of course you must keep to your game plan."

"And he might have gone to bed if I am late back from our meal." Why had she said that? It inferred they were going to stay out late. A wave of heat began to rise up her neck and she murmured "I'll see you there, at half six. Sorry, I'm busy, I have to go." She turned, willed her feet to take considered casual steps to the door and smothered the urge to bolt down the passage to the safety of her office. Had that gone as she'd planned? Moderately so, at least she hadn't buckled to his every request. Damn the man for being so attractive.

Andrew carried the tray holding their order of chicken and chips and navigated his way through the red-topped tables with their bolted-to-the-floor chairs and bright chrome trims. He led Antonia to the booths that lined the outside walls; more private and the bench seats looked a little more comfortable. He placed the tray on the dividing table and stood back, letting Antonia choose where to sit, then sat opposite her.

There was a stiffness in the atmosphere between them and once they'd eaten, he'd try to warm and bend the conversation. How many ways could he say sorry? Perhaps he'd ask her that – it might thaw the frost in her body language.

A short time later he said, "You were right. It's a tasty meal. Nice chips." He offered her the last few chips, but she shook her head so he ate them, wiped his hands on the serviette and sat back, replete, and feasted his eyes on her beauty.

"Your auburn hair is just lovely. Where do you get it from? Mother or father's side?"

"Don't know." She sipped the last of her drink, the straw drawing bubbles through the ice cubes like a muffled repeater gun. "I'm adopted." He wasn't quite sure how to comment on that, so waited. "Dad said I looked like an angel with an orange halo when I was a baby—but he's rather biased." Another suck on the straw, then she carried on. "I was very lucky. I have loving parents and Dad and I are very close. Mother can be a bit acerbic at times, but she means well. She's one of those people who put their mouth into gear before they engage their brain." The corner of her mouth lifted in a wry smile.

"How do you feel about being adopted?" A moment stretched into a pause, then into a longer gap until he wondered if he'd upset her with his question. His first really personal query and it seemed he'd blown it, but he waited, determined to force her to answer. When she began to talk, he had to lean forward to catch her words, her voice soft and hesitant while she twisted her serviette into a crumpled tube.

"I've always felt as if my birth mother abandoned me, probably because I looked ugly with a mop of red hair, red skinned and wrinkled. Perhaps she didn't think that—but it's what it felt like all of my life." She sighed, "I think being adopted and knowing it from a young age has made me more determined to succeed." She placed the massacred tissue on the tray and looked at him. "I don't know why I'm telling you this. I've only talked about it before, with my father." A waft of her perfume tickled his nose, just for a moment rising above the smell of fast food.

He wanted to kiss her there and then. Instead, he leaned back and said, "Perhaps no one has ever asked you the question before."

She inclined her head. "You're right. No one ever has. Saying it out loud has clarified my feelings. Perhaps I should stop striving so hard. What am I trying to prove? That I'm good enough?" Her fingers entwined to make a double fist. "I think it's the reason I often feel rejected or abandoned, because my mother did leave me." It sounded like something she'd said often.

He reached and touched her hands, risking a brief stroke of her fingers. "Perhaps she had no option. I'm sure she didn't want to. Have you considered that?"

She nodded, "But whatever the reasons, she left me."

His heart twisted at her sorrow, but there was little he could do to remedy this long-time hurt. He changed tack, as you would when sailing. "There's nothing wrong with striving. I do it all the time. It's learning when to stop that is the hard lesson." She rewarded him with a smile and at that moment, the ice thawed and they became acquaintances again. Not quite friends, but nearly. Seizing the moment he said, "In line with learning how to stop striving how about we go skiing this coming weekend?" She opened her mouth to reply, but he hurried on before she could. "I belong to a ski club that has a chalet, with bunks and a communal dining area. We can stay there overnight. I'll hire the skis so all you'll need is warm clothing. It's only a two-hour drive to the mountains from here and the ski fields opened last weekend." He held her gaze. "Please, Antonia. How many ways do I have to say sorry before you'll forgive me?"

She smiled and this time it reached her eyes. "I forgive you, Andrew, but please, even if the truth hurts don't ever lie to me again."

A surge of achievement lifted his spirits and he clapped his hands above his head in a fist of success.

"That doesn't mean I trust you yet, only that I forgive you the lies. You will have to work harder for my trust." Her statement softened by her smile.

"I will, I promise - and the ski trip? Are we friends and can we start all over again? Will you come?"

"Yes, I'll come. I have warm clothing here, at home. I'll email you my address and you can collect me on Friday evening. You'll have to satisfy Mother's curiosity and you can meet my lovely Dad." She slid out of the booth and he quickly joined her. "I'm going home now. I have a busy day tomorrow; then Thursday and Friday I'll have Judge Harding's decisions to process." She swept a stray auburn lock from her face and for a moment looked tired. "A weekend on the snowfields sounds like a lovely reward." She stood on tiptoe and her lips brushed his cheek. "Bye for now, thanks for the meal and your company. See you Friday, my friend."

He watched her walk away, weaving through the tables until she reached the entrance where she paused, raised her hand and beamed at him. He touched his cheek, his fingertips searching for evidence of her kiss. For the first time in years a spark of happiness lodged in his heart like an ember in a fire grate. Could this beautiful lady be the answer to his frozen emotions?

Chapter Six

"Dad, I'd like you to meet Andrew." She turned to him. "Andrew, this is my father."

"Good morning, Mr Prebble, pleased to meet you." Andrew waited as her father struggled to stand, waving away her move to assist him, and once steady he grasped Andrew's hand. "I hear you like a good game of chess?"

Her father nodded and indicated Andrew should sit in a nearby chair. Her father raised his eyebrows and pointed to the chessboard. "Yes, I do play occasionally," Andrew said, "but we really don't have time today. Perhaps another time we could share a game, if your daughter lets me come again." He grinned at Antonia and she frowned in mock consideration.

"Perhaps. We'll see," she said.

"I've made the coffee," her mother said, carrying the tray laden with coffee, mugs and biscuits into the sunroom. Antonia moved the chessboard and pieces to make room for the tray. An awkward silence swirled as they took their seats around the low table. Her mother fussed, filled and handed out the mugs. "So Mr. Maletto, you intend taking Antonia up to the snowfields for the weekend. Do you ski often?"

"Whenever I can, during the season." He bathed her mother with a charming smile and sipped his coffee. Antonia watched the interplay wondering what her mother would come out with next—and then it arrived. "Can we assume that this will be a naughty weekend or are your intentions honorable?" Only her mother would be this blunt. What would he say?

"Actually, whatever my deeper instincts may be, I intend to be totally honorable this weekend." He turned and winked at Antonia. She clenched her jaw to prevent a comment escaping. Her mother opened her mouth, but Andrew continued. "I can't be more honest than that. We will be staying in a dormitory with bunks and I expect everyone will be far too exhausted to be naughty." He said this dead-pan, not a smirk visible. "Will you release your daughter into my care? I promise to return her safe and sound – and un-tampered with." It seemed her mother had met her match in repartee because for a moment she didn't have an answer.

"Actually, I'm over the age of consent." Antonia said and picked up the plate. "Biscuit, Andrew?" She met her mother's gaze and saw concern and love in her eyes, belied by the firm set of her mouth. "I'll be just fine, Mother. I haven't skied since we all went to the snow five years ago, but I'm sure it's like riding a bicycle, I expect I'll pick it up again quite quickly." Her mother patted her knee and murmured, "Of course you will. Just be careful. I can't look after two invalids."

It sounded wrong, but Antonia knew her mother wasn't complaining about looking after her father, just worried that Antonia might have an accident. "We probably need to get going otherwise the day will be lost just getting there." She stood, "I'll just get my bag and put on a windbreaker," and she hurried away, leaving Andrew unprotected against her mother's curiosity. Obviously he could cope very well.

The ski lodge more than lived up to Andrew's description. The oblong building was divided in half. At one end was a dormitory of bunks and the other half housed a large living area with a kitchen and dining table on one side. The ablutions were in the middle between the living areas. At the end of the communal room a large open fire burned and the smell of Manuka oil from the flaming logs pervaded the air, canceling out the odor of fish and chips. A party of six had arrived just at dusk with this offering to add to the spaghetti bolognaise and four salads that had graced the dining table. Everyone sat around, either at the dining table, or collapsed into the ancient sofas that squatted in front of the fire like three large leather mouths, gasping for warmth. Every time someone came in from outside a chorus of 'shut the door' rang out. By the entrance a row of hooks supported damp ski clothes with boots lined beneath. The occasional waft of damp wool and drying boots moved into the main room moments after anyone entered. The chill of the mountain was only just being kept at bay by the insulated walls and double-glazed windows.

The flames in the fire grate held Antonia's gaze, hypnotizing her for moments on end. She blinked and let her mind roam over memories of the afternoon's skiing. After an initial hour on the nursery slopes the skill of skiing had returned and she'd ventured higher with each run. But not as high as Andrew, who, after checking she was managing had asked if she'd mind if he took the top ski lift and had a good run down the mountain. The old sensation of abandonment swamped her as she watched him glide away toward the chairlift, but she remembered his comments and tried to think of the struggle her birth mother must have gone through to give her up. The lonely feeling dissipated and she returned to the joy of skiing the slopes.

They'd met again by the ski hire shop at the arranged time and after returning their equipment had driven to the lodge further down the main road. She'd been introduced as his girlfriend and when she'd queried this in a quiet aside, he'd said, "Well, you're here, you're a girl and you're my friend." She really didn't have an answer to that. Perhaps he meant what he said and it didn't have any romantic connotations. A pity, because despite trying very hard not to succumb to his charms she found him good company. The tenseness in his movements and speech had eased. He smiled readily and so far there hadn't been a bout of silence.

But she wasn't going to accept this as the new norm. Anything could trigger a sulk, like the silence he'd retreated into at their picnic. But was it really a sulk? He hadn't acted like a child deprived of a favorite toy, or refused a treat. He didn't pout, or stomp his feet, or even scowl. He'd just retreated behind a wall of silence. She suspected it could be something deeper than a hangover from childhood, but until he voluntarily explained, on principle, she refused to ask.

Now, full of food and contentment, she struggled to stay awake. Muscles unused for years had been woken, stretched and used. She doubted she'd be able to walk in the morning.

The old couch moved as Andrew stretched his arm across the back of the sofa and eased it lightly down on to her shoulders. She was acutely aware of his thigh next to hers, his scent, musky with a hint of deodorant, excited her. Just as well he had honorable intentions, especially with the lodge full of people, but no one had asked her if she had honorable intentions and she smiled at the thought.

"Happy?" he said.

"Yes, blissfully. I haven't had so much fun for years. I might have to spend tomorrow in bed; I don't know if I'll be able to move in the morning."

"You'll be fine. Nothing that a hot shower won't fix. There's a large hot water cylinder and the fire is heating the water as we speak. Why not shower before you go to bed to loosen your muscles?"

She nodded. "Good idea, except I'm loathed to leave the fire. It's a joy after the flat and its central heating."

"Nothing beats an open fire," he said. "There's something romantic about it." His hug tightened around her and she leaned into his chest, her head resting against his shoulder. Her hair moved and her scalp tingled as he dropped a kiss on her head.

"In the firelight your hair is gleaming red. It's beautiful," he murmured in her ear, "And so are you."

"Thank you." What more could she say? She knew he was telling the truth, as he saw it, even if she didn't quite believe him. But he had promised not to lie, so perhaps he was right? Maybe it was time to consider her hair color an asset instead of a nuisance. Then she gave up thinking and enjoyed the warmth, the company, and the camaraderie of a group of people all mad on skiing. The in-house jokes went over her head and Andrew would whisper into her ear what so-and-so meant and what event had triggered the teasing. She didn't feel left out. In fact, be the time they all stood and decided to go to bed, she knew she'd made some good friends. A few leading questions had been avoided because she really didn't know where she stood with Andrew. This weekend's girlfriend, or more than that? She smiled and agreed to the group's future plans. Easier to do that than qualify her presence tonight.

In the morning the mountain called. As dawn crept over the distant hills, first one bunk creaked, then another, and soon all beds were empty as sleepers rose, fed, rugged up and left for the slopes. Each person set on extracting every minute they could from the white slopes, stumbling with stiff joints, laughing in expectation, ramming gear into cars now so they could ski until the last moment before they had to leave and return to their boring day jobs.

Despite her previous misgivings, Antonia found she could move freely, after all. She woke refreshed and ready to tackle the higher slopes today. In the showers the three other women nattered with the ease of old friends and she washed and dressed as quickly as she could, avoiding their curiosity. It appeared she was the first woman Andrew had ever brought to the lodge and rather than admit she hardly knew him, she brushed off their queries using time as an excuse and hurried outside to load the car.

She stood and inhaled the smell of fresh snow. Overnight, the mountains had been dusted again and the air had a crisp, almost peppermint, odor to it. Her nostrils tickled with the cold and she rubbed the end of her nose with her gloved hand.

"When do we need to leave? What time do you need to be back in the city?"

"I'd like to stay here for another week," he said, "but you have work and so do I. I've got the monthly partner's meeting on Wednesday afternoon and heaps of clients booked in over the week. Arbitration never sleeps," he chuckled, "It just keeps on percolating until a compromise is found. Often I'm the one that finds it."

"You must be good at it. That's a skill not many people have," she said, pushing her bag firmly into the corner of the trunk. "Seeing things from both sides and finding the middle ground isn't always easy. That's how wars are started."

He laughed. "Yes, that's what I'm dealing with mini-wars and skirmishes, without the knives and guns." He closed the trunk. "Right, let's drive to the parking area, get geared up and hit the slopes." He lifted her and swung her around. "I'm having a ball. Thanks so much for coming." He stood her carefully down on the gravel and snowflakes, and held her a moment or two longer than necessary to ensure she had her balance, then leaned closer and kissed her. Surprise pulled her back for a second before she leaned in and responded to his lips, warm and gentle as they covered hers; his tongue flickered, hesitant and requesting, until she relented and fell into the kiss. Long moments later they parted, breathless, she a little embarrassed by the passion that had risen from the depths of her being. Had he noticed?

"Very nice," he said, "I could do with more of that—but not just now." He smiled, his gaze locked with hers, "Perhaps later?" She nodded. Yes, later would be great. She needed a few more kisses like that. An ideal way to build trust and banish doubt.

"Right, look out snow, here we come." He grasped her

hand and hurried her to the passenger door, opened it for her then ran around to the other side, bounced into the driver's seat and started the car. He reminded her of a puppy let off its leash. No his tongue wasn't hanging out and he wasn't panting; but his eyes were sparkling, his movements fluid and he seemed to be suppressing a dynamo of energy. Laughter lines creased his cheeks and he even whistled as he drove up the road to the snowfields.

By midday she'd had enough physically. "I can't ski another yard. Truly, I have to stop."

A wistful look flashed across his face. They stood next to the chairlift after their last downhill run.

"Haven't you had enough?" She grinned because he had that look again, of a small boy about to be taken off the slopes. "If we don't have to go yet, then you do another run and I'll wait here."

"You don't mind?" He cocked his head. "Truly, because I will be a while by the time I get up the top, wait for a gap in the downhill traffic and ski back. Could be at least an hour."

"Of course I don't mind." She pointed to the hire shop and the cafe next door. "I'll be in there, drinking coffee and resting my legs."

"Right. Good girl. Thanks." He beckoned her closer. Did he have a final instruction? She slid her ski's alongside his. He crooked his finger and she leaned closer. "Gotcha," and he hugged her with one arm and kissed her lightly on the cheek, then dug into his pockets, "Here're the car keys. Better get your jacket. Once you've stopped exercising, you'll cool down. Might get a chill. See you soon." Before she could reply he'd skied away to line up for the next chairlift seat. She raised her arm in salute and crossed to the hire-shop to return her gear. At the doorway to the café, she watched the line of chairlift seats travel up the mountain, over the first ridge to disappear only to reappear as tiny smudges further up the mountain. Again, that abandonment sensation crept into her chest and she batted it down, determined not to let it spoil her day. It returned with a vengeance when he didn't come back. After an hour she retrieved their jackets from the car and waited some more.

Two hours later he still hadn't arrived. She wandered out onto the deck and watched as a group of men in high-viz vests set off up the mountain in two snowmobiles. "Another injured skier," the man next to her said, nodding toward the departing crew. Hopefully not Andrew, but where was he?

By the time the snowmobiles returned, she was on her way to the administration office to report him missing, now worried she'd left it too late. The weather was closing in. Someone called her name and she turned to see one of the rescue crew hurrying toward her.

"Miss Prebble?"

"Yes, that's me. Is it Andrew?" Her stomach twisted into a knot. "I've been so worried." She followed the man to a bright yellow boat affair, shaped a bit like a banana, and they're strapped in lay Andrew, his face gray and drawn.

"Hi," he said "Twisted my damn knee, can't put it to the ground. Shocking pain." He seemed to drift off, his gaze wandering past her to focus on the distance.

"He's full of painkillers," the man said as if to explain Andrew's vagueness. "We're taking him to the Accident and Emergency Department by ambulance, Miss, Can you follow?"

Where were the car keys? She fumbled in the pockets of Andrew's jacket and found them. "Yes, I'll follow you." It wasn't as if she didn't know how to drive, she just didn't do it all that often. Like skiing, she guessed the skill would come back to her quite quickly once she got going. At least, following an ambulance, she should be safe. Just the sight of an ambulance seemed to make people drive carefully.

_____//_____

The murmur of other patients filtered through the dividing curtains in the emergency rooms, punctuated by the occasional curse or sharp intake of breath. Antonia sat beside the bed and held Andrew's hand. A sense of uselessness weighed on her shoulders. The weekend's activities were beginning to tell. Her limbs ached, her spine wanted to bend and stop supporting her head, which presently hosted a brain kept alert only by the smell of antiseptic and alcohol rub. Andrew's face had lost the gray tinge, stubble had appeared on his chin and his hair hung lank over his forehead, damp from perspiration. He leaned back, propped on the bed, his leg supported over a pillow. His knee had been X-rayed and they awaited the results.

The curtain swished open and the Registrar pulled it closed behind him. The loops skidded with a high pitch screech along the metal rod and set her teeth on edge.

"Good news and bad news," he said. He looked as tired as Andrew. "The good news is that there are no fractures. All bones accounted for and correct." He smiled and held Andrew's wrist, possibly taking his pulse as he paused. "The bad news is that you have an ACL. You've torn the anterior cruciate ligament. This will need an operation to fix it, plus weeks of recovery post-op' and possibly six to nine months before you'll be skiing again." He placed Andrew's arm back on his lap and patted his shoulder. "We'll put a brace around your knee for traveling and I'll get the physio to come shortly and set you up with a pair of crutches." He noted something on a clipboard and asked Antonia, "Can you take him home? He can't drive."

"Not a problem," she said, having already assumed this would be necessary if they let him go.

"Right then. I'll arrange the discharge papers which you can take to your orthopedic surgeon as soon as possible. You will need pain relief until surgery and lots of rest.

Meanwhile, enjoy what's left of your weekend," he said, smiled and left them alone once more.

An hour later they stood in the car park. Darkness cloaked them, but the moon lit the mountains on the horizon, painting a white band beneath the indigo sky. Stars sparkled and wavered in the chill air. Antonia held open the passenger's door and waited as Andrew sat, then eased his injured leg into the car. Conversation seemed to be beyond him, but his color had improved. She drove them out of the car park and onto the main highway, heading for home. Tomorrow she'd take a sick day from work and drive him back to the city.

The road twisted around the lake with hairpin bends and short straights which were overhung with trees. Down from the high altitude they drove into a storm and the rain set in. The car floated over the road and she had to concentrate. The lightest touch on the accelerator and the wheels responded, but eventually she learned what pressure to apply and didn't need to brake so often. Cars whizzed past her on the straights, tired of following her at below the speed limit. She didn't care. All that mattered was to get him safely home. Leaves hit the windscreen then disappeared instantly, only to be followed by more. Some stuck under the base of wiper blades. She'd need to clear them. They glowed red and yellow in the headlights of the oncoming cars. Pretty, but a hazard all the same.

At the next small settlement, where a few streetlights dotted the highway, she pulled into the shoulder and stopped. She glanced across and in the weak sodium glow saw him wipe his cheek. He'd only made the occasional smothered moan in the last ten minutes.

Time to have a rest. She could do with a break. Night driving wasn't much fun. She turned off the motor and reached for his hand.

His fingers were wet. Blood? Was he bleeding? She

fumbled, found the switch and turned on the inside light. He turned to her with a weak smile. "I'm such a bad passenger, especially at night." His tears had left a trail down his cheeks. "It's not your fault. I'm always terrified if someone else drives."

"I didn't think I was that bad a driver." The joke fell flat. He shook his head in the tiniest of no's. She reached and pulled him against her chest, his head resting on her breasts. "You should have told me. Shall I find somewhere for us to stay the night? Is there anywhere nearby?"

He searched and found her hand and gripped it tight. "No truly, it's not your driving; it's my memories that terrify me."

"Sometimes talking about it helps. Can you do that? People tell me I'm a good listener." She stroked his head and brushed his hair off his face. "Only if you want to, otherwise we will just stay here until you feel better." Several minutes passed and she began to wonder if she should break their embrace and restart the car. It wasn't the most comfortable embrace she'd experienced, but it certainly had the most emotion swirling around it. There would be accommodation in the small towns they had yet to pass through. She would drive until she found somewhere. His voice quiet and hesitant broke into her thoughts.

"A drunk motorist drove into our car one night. He killed my parents and my dog. I was strapped into the back seat and dozing. My father's shouted curse woke me, then headlights lit the inside of our car and an almighty crash pushed us off the road. The car rolled down a bank. Over and over –and over."

He stopped speaking. Was that it? Then he began again, his voice a little stronger. "Dad's chest was crushed by the steering wheel. Mum had her neck broken and my dog flew out a window. I survived—totally alone in the dark."

Another silence, not quite so long this time. "I couldn't

get out of my seatbelt. I listened to Dad's death rattle, while my dog howled in pain nearby. All I had was a broken nose." His voice broke and he took a shuddering breath. "The drunk drove on but eventually a car stopped because our headlights shone into the trees below the road/"

"Shhh, you're safe," she murmured. "I'm here. It's all right."

"I still get nightmares and relive the crash again and again. Everyone dies except me. Lots of car crashes. Complete strangers die in them, but I always survive and wake up."

"That must be awful. No wonder you're a bad passenger."

"Worst of all I still want to kill the man that killed my family. I could murder him quite easily and that frightens me."

She didn't have an answer to that. More minutes passed before he sat up and kissed her cheek. "You're a darling. Sorry to toss all that on you. I'm usually quite stoic about it. Must be the painkillers making me all emotional."

"Nonsense, it's totally understandable after the day you've had with your accident and all the pain." She rested her hand on his thigh above the brace. "Now I'm going to turn off the light, start the car and drive you carefully home to Mother, who will just love having a handsome man to put to bed."

He gave a small laugh. "I bet."

"She will, she'll love it. It proves she was right. One of us got injured, so her feelings were correct." As they moved off, she added, "And tomorrow I'm going to drive you back to the city and take you home, so this flash car can be put in its garage before another car kisses it. I'll go back to the flat for the night and come home again on Tuesday; once I've made sure you're able to get to a doctor." She started the motor, glanced to see he had his lips clenched. "I suggest you close your eyes, Andrew. That way you can't see what's going on and you probably need to sleep."

Which he did, and she suspected he slept most of the way. Certainly he was asleep when she and her mother woke him to get him out of the car. Perhaps sharing his fears had eased their potency.

Hot drinks, a bowl of soup, followed by the story of how some idiot had skied into him, totally out of control, had him smiling again. He'd broken the other fellow's fall and taken the force of the collision, landing in the snow with the other man tangled on top of him. Passing skiers had phoned the mountain rescue team, but it had taken them ages to get to him and transport him down. "Totally embarrassing to arrive on the banana boat," he said and hoped none of the lodge's residents had witnessed it. He would be stuck with some nickname forever if they had. By the time they all went to bed, his tension had eased. She never said a word about his fear of night driving. A banana-boat ride and a damaged knee were probably enough embarrassments for one day.

By morning Andrew had recovered his cheeky grin and energy. He rose early, showered and spent an hour with her father, playing chess. She rang the district court and took two days off, citing Andrew's injury and using some of her holiday leave. Having extra hours in the city, without racing back home, meant she could visit the flat and see her friends. They'd want a progress report. Had there been any progress? Yes, there had been. Quite a lot. He'd trusted her with his deepest fears and she would return the compliment by not repeating them. If he trusted her then she would trust him too. It must have been very hard to give up his secret. But she would give the girls a blow by blow account of everything else.

When she suggested they leave, feeling the day frittering away, he arranged to text his next move to her father, so they could continue to play the game. As well he suggested a couple of websites her father could join to play chess with others. Language wasn't necessary, only the game's moves mattered. His acts of kindness touched her.

"Thank you for playing chess with Dad, and getting him onto those internet sites. I don't know why I never thought of it. Perhaps, a bit selfishly, I wanted it to be something only he and I did. He desperately needs the stimulation."

"It's my privilege. I miss my Dad. I'm being selfish borrowing yours." And that was the only reference to his revelations of the night before.

Today she had a better handle on the car and its spirited performance. She navigated the city's streets under Andrew's guidance and pulled the car into the driveway of a two-story home, in one of the better suburbs. What a posh residence. The high wrought iron gates had swung open with a touch of a button on the console. She parked under the portico and admired the plane tree in the middle of the lush smooth lawn. A circular carpet of leaves dressed the base, a riot of orange, yellow and red. The tips of the branches were bare, but two-thirds of the tree's leaves clung on. The sun shone through the clouds at that moment to light the tree as if in a spotlight on the stage and turned the remaining leaves into a ball of color.

"So beautiful," she murmured, and remembered to turn off the motor.

"Yes, you are."

She turned to find him gazing at her and in a moment of confusion asked, "Home Sweet Home?"

"Yes, but it's just a house now. Somewhere to sleep, eat and unwind in between work."

"You're not going to get much work done in the next few days," she said and uncertain what to do next she hurried to the trunk and retrieved his case, then made sure he had his short crutches in his hands so he could get out of the car.

She carried his bag and stood beside him as he sorted

the house key from the collection on the car's key ring. Through the open door, she saw a grand staircase climbed from the entrance lobby and turned out of sight. "I hope you can sleep on the ground floor. Those stairs might be a bit much."

"There's an elevator in that cupboard," he said, pointing to a door nearby. "Mother needed it, before the accident." He mentioned his mother, another good sign.

"If you show me where the garage is, I'll open the door and put the car away." Uncertainty filled her. After being in charge since yesterday, suddenly her job was over. "Then perhaps you could ring for a taxi for me?"

He dropped his crutches. They clattered on the marble tiled floor. He spread his arms, wavering a little as he balanced on one foot and one big toe. "Antonia, don't go yet." He spread his arms. The invitation to step into his embrace caught her by surprise and then she remembered their kiss on Sunday morning. Was it just yesterday? So much had happened. She hesitated.

"Please." His gaze locked with hers, his eyes filled with longing, pleaded. "You can't go, just like that. There's food in the pantry, wine in the cellar."

None of that mattered to her, and then he added, "Besides, I love you and I don't want you to go."

Well, that made a huge difference and she stepped into his embrace. She didn't want to go either. His lips covered hers and emotion flowed like molten lava until he broke their kiss. "If you pass me my crutches, I think I can make the elevator."

She watched as he adjusted his stance with the crutches at his side and stood as erect as he could manage. After a grimace of pain an air of formality dropped over him and his mouth tightened. "I'm overcome with weak knees and need to lie down upstairs. Will you join me, Miss Prebble? I might need to give some dictation." For a moment, disappointment flipped her stomach. He wanted her to take dictation? Then one corner of his mouth titled with a suppressed smile. He was role-playing and teasing her.

She laughed. "I'd be delighted to join you, Mr Maletto," she said, trying hard to keep a straight face. "I've the whole day free. I'm yours until this evening."

In the lift he kissed her again and whispered, "I'd like you to be mine for more than today. How about tomorrow and forever? Do you have space in your diary?"

"I'll check. The Judge might have other plans, but I can probably squeeze you in."

"I'll make it worth your while. I can offer better surroundings, less pressure and endless nights of love. I bet the judge can't match that?"

The role-playing ceased as he kissed her again. His tongue probed and she relented. He tasted of chestnuts and chocolate. His scent excited her and the warmth of his love promised joyous security. They ignored the sound of the lift's door opening and closing reminding them they had arrived upstairs.

She knew she had arrived at a turning point in her life and if this was love, then it promised to be more fun than she'd ever dreamed of.

I'll Never Let You Fall
Cynthia Staton

Summary

It was love at first sight. It just had to be as Daniel saw her for the first time. Nothing else mattered after that as he pursued the one he knew had to be meant for him.

Biography

Cynthia Staton has a novel, *Life Lived Not Lost: A Journey of Hope* and is in several anthologies. She has found out that she, too, has the love for writing fiction as much as she does nonfiction.

I'll Never Let You Fall
Cynthia Staton

Almost three weeks ago I started attending classes at college. I was accepted at many different colleges as I received letter after letter, day after day. I prayed for guidance in making my decision. I was drawn to one college in particular. I knew it was my destiny to attend Messiah College in Mechanicsburg. I am working on getting my bachelor's in history. History has always been my greatest subject all throughout my school years. I have given much thought to becoming a history teacher or professor. I would even love to open a history museum one day. But that's a whole different story for now.

So, here I am, walking across the campus. It's a cold November day, and of course, I forgot my coat in my dorm. Luckily, the classroom is only a short walk. I walked into the classroom and took my seat. I looked at the history professor at the front of the room. I have only known him for a few weeks, but I already admire him. He is as serious about history as I am. I knew I would learn a lot from Professor Dawson and I was excited about our major assignment. We had to choose any historical figure and write, or should I say type ten thousand to twenty-five thousand words about this person. It was due by the end of term and was a huge part of our final grade. I was researching and taking notes every chance, I got. I spent a lot of time in the library or on my computer in my dorm. I never did much besides study. I didn't even give much, if any, thought about love. So, I was nowhere near ready when it happened today.

After class, I was walking back across the campus, going back to my dorm. Later in the afternoon, I would attend drama class in the auditorium. Acting was my second interest. I would love to act in history-related movies and reenactments. That would be awesome. So, again, here I am walking, with my nose in my history book, when I am almost knocked backward. At least I kept her from falling to the ground. Obviously, she didn't see the patch of ice. So, there I stood, holding this young woman who was now looking up at me. I stood her up. No, not like that, I mean we haven't even officially met. I eased her back upright, so she could stand on her own.

"Oh, um thankyouimsorry," was how it came out of her mouth.

"Uh, no problem," I said. "Are you alright?"

"Yes, I am fine," she answered.

It sounds kind of weird, I know, but we just stood there staring at each other. I suddenly realized that she was so beautiful.

"My name is Daniel," I broke the strange silence.

"Oh, I'm Angelica," she told me. "Or just Angel."

"I'll see you around, I guess," I told her.

"Sure," she said.

As I walked away, I turned around to steal another glance. I knew I was not in her league, but there was just something about her. I was not even supposed to be looking for love. History was on my mind, not love. I decided to just try to push it out of my mind, but that proved almost impossible. In fact, that would not be the last time I saw her that day.

That afternoon, I headed to the auditorium for drama. Professor Jackson talked about what we should expect in the class. Also, what she expected from us. I found it impossible to focus on her words, which was not like me at all. I always took school seriously. Her face kept flashing through my mind. No, not Professor Jackson's face. Sheesh, she had to be at least fifty. I kept thinking of…okay I'll say it…the woman of my dreams.

After class, I headed straight for the library. I had

decided to do my paper about Martin Luther King, Jr. I was very fascinated by him. I picked out some books and went to sit when she called out to me. Sort of.

"Oh, Darryl, hi," she said.

I realized I was standing right in front of her table. "It's Daniel," I corrected her.

"Oh, sorry," she blushed.

"Oh, it's alright," I attempted to brush it off.

There was that strange silence as we stared at each other again.

"You can sit down, if you want," she broke the silence this time.

I took a seat across the table from her.

"So, how are you?" I asked, trying to make conversation.

"I am fine," she smiled. "I am researching for my history assignment."

"Same with me," I responded.

I couldn't believe it, but I decided to press my luck.

"Maybe we can hang out sometime," I suggested.

"I would like that," she said.

She must feel the strange connection too, I thought.

"I have to go," I said. "I have to work tomorrow."

"Okay," she responded, "See you later, then."

Although this was only the second time I saw her, I felt like I wanted to kiss her.

I went back to my dorm. Usually, I would study while I ate dinner, but I was in no studying mood and did not feel like my normal self. Was I in love? I couldn't be. Could I? This was unbelievable. We had agreed to see each other again. But when? And where? I had no idea. I barely knew her, yet I could not stop thinking about her. I wondered if I would even be able to sleep that night. Or ever again for that matter. I finished half my dinner, hardly able to focus on food, much less anything else. Was this love? I just wasn't sure. I had never fallen in love. I mean, okay, I have had little crushes when I was younger, but so what? I showered, then went to bed that night, unsure I would even be able to sleep.

The next morning, I woke up to the sound of my phone ringing. "Hello, Mom," I answered.

"Hello, Daniel," she replied, "How are you?"

"Oh, fine, Mom," I said, "Just getting ready for work." "How are you and Dad?"

"We are doing great. We just really miss you a lot!" she said. "Oh, well, we are all snowed in here—," Mom began.

I just could not focus on her words. In fact, I didn't actually hear anything else for what must have been at least several minutes, though it seemed like an eternity.

"Daniel? Are you there?" I realized Mom was trying to get my attention.

"Oh, yeah," I said. "I am still half-asleep."

"I was just saying that Dad and I will have to delay our trip to see you," she told me, "Due to the weather and the road conditions."

"Uh, yeah, no problem, that's fine," I tried to sound more disappointed. Not that I wasn't disappointed, but it seemed I could only focus on Angelica right now. *I know*, I thought, *I will ditch work and go find her.*

"Talk to you later, Daniel. Dad and I love you," Mom interrupted my thoughts again.

"I love you too, bye," I said and then hung up.

I went back to my thoughts about going to find Angelica. But, I knew that was silly. I already told her I was working today. Besides, we just met and have only spoken twice. I mean, she might think I am creepy or something. Almost an hour later, I pulled into the driveway of the local bowling alley. I had worked at the Bowl-A-Rama for three years now. My hours had been adjusted since I had started college, but at least I still had a job. Lately, we had not been too busy. Especially since tournament season had ended after the summer. I worked behind the counter, taking admission payments and handing out shoes. I know, I know, a typical job at a bowling alley. About halfway through my shift, something very amazing happened. She walked in. Angelica came in with some other girls.

"I don't think I have seen you here before," I said when she walked up to the counter.

"Yes, I usually stay in, but my sorority sisters insisted I get out," she responded.

"Oh, a sorority." I was a little taken aback. But I quickly remembered we had never talked about where we lived.

"Yes, Gamma Phi Beta," she told me. "Or Gamma Phi for short."

"Awesome," I replied. "Well, uh, welcome to Bowl-A-Rama."

"Thanks," she smiled shyly.

The other girls joined her, and I gave them all their shoes. "Have fun," I said to neither of them in particular.

Seconds later, Angelica returned to the counter. "Can we get a pitcher of coke and some glasses?" she asked.

"Absolutely," I answered her, "I will bring it right over."

Angelica and her friends bowled for nearly two hours before returning their shoes.

"Bye, Daniel," she said as she left.

"Bye, baby," I replied before I could stop myself.

"What?" She stopped in her tracks.

"Uh, uh, yeah, I will see you later," I tried to push it off.

She smiled and walked out the door.

Whew, I thought, *that was close*. But, I had saved the moment. I hoped I did anyway. I tried not to think about it. Although, in a way, I did not exactly regret that I had said it. Other than I was sure I sounded like an idiot. I finished my shift, helped close up and then I drove home. I was supposed to work the next day too, but I just had to see her.

The next day I got up, ate a little breakfast, and then

paced my dorm room until noon. Then I set off for the library. I hoped she would be there. I was disappointed though, as there was no sign of her. I pretended to browse the books for almost an hour, hoping she would come in. I finally decided to just leave. I wondered where else to look. It was Sunday, so obviously there were no classes today. But there was choir practice. Maybe, just maybe, she takes choir. So, I walked into the music room. I peered in at all the faces who were busy singing. There was no sign of her. I left again, disappointed. I wanted to find her. I just needed to. But where was she today? I could not go check the bowling alley, since I had called in sick. I didn't think it was likely she would be there anyway. I mean, who bowled two days in a row? Much less more than once during a week. Then something occurred to me. Gamma Phi Beta. That was it. But I couldn't just show up to her sorority, could I? I mean, I would have to have a reason. I could ask her to study with me, I considered. Almost right away, that sounded stupid, even in my mind. I mean, it was not very likely that we were doing our paper on the same person. Although, she did say she was working on history the other night at the library. So then, I argued with myself, we could still study together. Couldn't we? I was not sure what exactly I decided. All I knew was I was suddenly standing in front a sorority house reading the letters. Gamma Phi Beta. Gamma Phi, for short, she had said. Then I was actually ringing the bell.

"Can I help you?" One of her friends answered the door.

"Uh," I said, "Is Angelica here?"

"Sorry, she spends Sundays with her parents," she said. "Every Sunday," she added.

"Oh, uh, no problem," I told her. "Would you tell her I came by?"

"Sure," she shrugged.

"Right, um, bye then," I muttered. I left without any further exchange of words. It was kind of weird, though, I was feeling half relieved, half disappointed. I had called in from work, hoping to hang out with Angelica. I had nothing to do with my day now. Okay, so that was not really true, because yes, I was going to spend it studying and writing my history paper. I decided to pick up a pizza on the way back to my dorm. When I got home, I grabbed my laptop, my history work, and turned the history channel on TV. They were showing a documentary on the life of Martin Luther King, Jr. *What luck*, I thought. Maybe even a little coincidental. I watched the whole three-hour show as I worked on my paper. After the show ended and I had decided to stop working on my paper, I put a few slices of pizza in the microwave for dinner. I did not feel much like cooking anyway. I went to sleep that night with high hopes of seeing Angelica sometime the next day. As I fell asleep, I wondered if I should buy her some flowers. Perhaps it was too soon for that, I decided.

The next morning, I headed to history class, and for the first time in my whole life, I was anxious for class to end. Yes, I am shocked about that, too. By the end of history class, I was also shocked that I barely even listened to Professor Dawson. I just couldn't focus. I know my studies should be the most important thing, especially because after college, I would go out to face the world. College depended on me having a good job rather than working some dead-end job at a burger joint or something like that. And yes, I know my parents would be disappointed in this behavior.

With class over, and it being near lunchtime, I decided to go to the university cafeteria. I was not really feeling very hungry, but I was assuming Angelica would not be in the library until later. Also, I had no idea what class she had in the mornings. The cafeteria food didn't look too appetizing (which is why I usually never ate there), so I just ordered a hot dog and some fries and a coke. The second reason I never ate here came when the cashier told me the total was almost ten dollars. What a waste, I thought as I sat down at an empty table. There was no way I was even going to consider buying dessert. At these prices, I would rather just go to the vending machine. I sort of hoped that Angelica might come in to eat, but no such luck. I finished eating and decided to just go to the library. I didn't have another class until later, and it wouldn't hurt to just see if she was there. I realize I make it sound as if she is avoiding me and I am hunting her down, but I am just so anxious to see her. I mean, I actually feel a need to see her. A thought suddenly struck me. I could go to her sorority house again and see if she is there. No, I almost instantly decided. Then she would almost definitely think I was a creep. A horrifying thought followed that realization. Maybe she already thought that after her friends told her I stopped by yesterday. Maybe that was why I had not seen her anywhere.

Running through my mind now was the thought that she actually is avoiding me. Suddenly nothing else mattered. I can't eat, drink, or anything else. I could not even think about my history paper right now, or my job for that matter. I was actually growing concerned. It was playing out in my mind, over and over again. Maybe she had heard me call her "baby" the other night at the bowling alley. She was probably angry or plain disgusted to find out that I actually went to her sorority house yesterday. Oh no! She must certainly think I'm a creep. Or even worse, she probably thinks I am a stalker. I suddenly wanted to fall in a hole and die. I hoped that I would at least get a chance to explain.

I went back to my dorm feeling both angry with myself and depressed. I got in the shower and just let the hot water run over my head. I had already decided not to even bother going to my afternoon drama class. There was no way I would pay attention anyway. I just did not care about anything else right now. I was not sure how long I stood in the shower. I had lost track of time. I got out, dried off and dressed. I wanted to go to the library. I doubted she was even there or that she would ever be there again. I grabbed my phone to call and say I could not make it in for my evening shift. The phone rang a few times.

"Hello, thank you for calling Bowl-A-Rama, my name is Victoria, how can I help you?" answered the shift manager, Victoria Thurman.

"Hey, Torrie, it's Daniel. I am a bit under the weather, I don't think I can work this evening," I lied.

"No problem, we aren't busy anyway," she replied. "Oh, I have a message for you. I wasn't here, but somebody came in looking for you. Dave believes she said her name was Angelique or something like that."

"Right, uh, thanks," I said then hung up. Okay, I know that was rude, but I am excited again. Angelica went looking for me at the bowling alley this morning!

However, just as suddenly, I was hit with that sinking feeling again. Duh, she went there to chew me out. To call me out as a creepy stalker guy. She wanted to put me in my place and tell me to stay away from her and that she never wanted to see or speak to me again. There was no doubt that was it. It had to be. Obviously, she wanted to give me hell in front of my coworkers. If I could just get a chance to explain and apologize, I thought gloomily. It was probably too late for that anyway.

I am not really sure why, but I decided to go to the library after all. I guess I just did not want to sit around in my dorm any more right now. I did not really want to study. I had no plans to do so either. I slumped into the library with my head hung low in both shame and low spirits. I walked over to the history section on impulse. Out of habit, you know. I pretended to scan the books on the shelves. I was just about to leave when the most unbelievable (yes, I know I am being dramatic) incident almost made me jump out of my shoes.

"Daniel!" she shrieked.

I turned around. She had her hand over her mouth, looking around as if expecting to be scolded for being too loud in the library.

"Angelica, uh, listen, please, I am so sorry," I started.

"Sorry for what?" she asked. She was smiling.

"You must have thought I was a creep, showing up to your sorority house and all," I shivered.

"I was so thrilled when Becca told me you came by," she beamed. "I went by the bowling alley this morning, but you were not there. I couldn't stop thinking of you," she added.

I was sure my jaw dropped to the floor with those words.

"I just have to tell you something," she went on, "I know this is crazy but—," she hesitated. Then somehow it just happened.

"I LOVE YOU!" we said at the same time. Then just like that, it seemed that time stood still. And then I decided I was not going to waste this moment. I took her in my arms and kissed her. It was the best moment of my life. So far, anyway. When we pulled apart, she was the first to speak.

"It has been so hard to talk to you," she said.

"Oh, yeah, I know, for real," I agreed. She looked at me with a beautiful smile.

"You called me 'baby' the other night at the bowling alley," she said rather shyly.

I nearly gasped when that came out of her mouth.

"Uh, yeah, just lost in the moment, I suppose," I offered.

"You took me by surprise," she laughed, "but I believe I felt the same thing you did."

"This connection is very amazing." I smiled. I decided to just go for it and ask the question on my mind.

"Can I take you out?" I asked. "I mean, I would really like to take you." I wanted it to sound sincere, because it was. I just hoped she believed me.

"I would love to," she accepted.

"How about next Friday night?" I suggested.

"That will be perfect," she said happily. We sat and studied together for another couple of hours. When we finished for the evening, I offered to drive her back to her sorority house. She accepted. We said goodbye, then I drove back toward my dorm.

I arrived home, feeling the best I had in what seemed like forever. I was very happy. The girl of my dreams was for real mine. She belonged to me, and now we have a date next Friday night. Where should I take her? Bowling? Not a chance. I smiled to myself. Unless she wanted to go, of course. I will take her to a movie and out for dinner. Maybe we will go visit the history museum. All I knew was that I could not wait to take her out on our very first date.

I awoke the next morning with a smile on my face. It was only Tuesday, but today was going to be much better than yesterday. I had no doubt about that. I was even able to focus in history class like I normally did. It still seemed to take forever for the day's lesson to end. I know now that there was something more important to me than even history. Yet, before meeting Angelica, I never gave much thought about finding love. Not even in high school. My education was all that ever mattered to me. I never really even hung out much either. I spent most afternoons studying.

After history class, I turned on my cell phone and dialed her number. I had already been planning on asking her to have lunch with me. I listened to the phone ringing on her end, just waiting for her to answer.

"Hello, Daniel," came her angelic voice. "How are you?"

"I am great," I responded. "Would you like to have lunch with me?"

"Oh," she sounded disappointed. "I have already gone for lunch with my sorority sisters. I didn't even think—I mean we are already—"

"Oh, that's fine," I tried to convince her. "It's no problem, really!"

"I will have lunch with you tomorrow!" she suggested.

"Yes, that will be great!" I exclaimed. "What class do you have in the morning?" I asked.

"My morning class is microbiology," she answered.

"Oh, cool," I said, perhaps too enthusiastically, "You are just right down the hall from me, then."

"Awesome, we will meet after class tomorrow, then." She sounded excited.

"Do you want to study tonight?" I asked her.

"I'm so sorry, I can't tonight," she apologized, "I am babysitting my little brother for my parents."

"Okay, that's fine, baby," I assured her.

"I love you, Daniel," she said.

"I love you too, baby," I responded. "I can't wait to see you tomorrow."

Although neither of us wanted to, we said bye and hung up.

I got in my car and decided to go get lunch from Burger Barn. In my opinion, the name of the burger joint was lame and the country hay barn style structure was out of date, but they had awesome burgers, so it was alright. I went through the drive-thru and ordered a double cheeseburger with fries and an ice cold coke. I got my order, then headed back to my dorm to pack in some major study time. Then I would be skipping drama class because I had to work. Right then, an idea occurred to me. I could call later and ask Angelica to visit me at the bowling alley. She could bring her little brother bowling. I would even give them a free pass. I knew Torrie wouldn't mind. She was a stern manager, but kind-hearted.

Just a short while later, I pulled up at Bowl-A-Rama, ready to begin my shift. I had told Torrie that I would work extra tonight to make up for lost time. I hadn't told her yet, but I was considering asking for more hours. All I would have to do is drop drama class. It wouldn't be that big of a deal...acting was not that important to me. As long as I got my degree in history, which there was no question that I would.

"Hey Daniel," Torrie greeted me, "How's your day?"

"It's great so far," I responded. "By the way, I am sorry I missed a couple days of work."

"Don't worry about it," she insisted. "But be ready, because this week we are doing ball inspections.

"Ball inspections?" I inquired.

"We are checking all the balls for cracks, scratches, and any damages and wears," she simplified. "I have a shipment of brand new balls coming in by next week."

"That's great!," I exclaimed.

"Yes," she agreed, "We are getting rid of the old ones." "After the new balls are in, we are going to celebrate with a buy one get one special on games for an entire week."

"That should get business rolling," I laughed.

Torrie snorted, trying not to burst out laughing. She would laugh at the silliest things. Even stupid little puns. She was easy to get along with.

At break time, I texted Angelica.

Daniel: Hey, babe! ♥□

Angelica: Hi, baby!! ☺☺ Aren't you in class??

Daniel: No, I skipped class to go to work early, and I wanted to ask you to come to see me here tonight. ☺☺

Angelica: I am not sure□□ with my little brother, you know.

Daniel: Oh, come on, bring him bowling. I am sure he will love it!!!!! 😄😄

Daniel: I can give you a free pass for tonight □□□

Angelica: Well, alright, I will be there shortly, but I can

only stay an hour, maybe an hour and a half because I have to get him in bed. My parents are picking him up in the morning.

Daniel: That's great!! I can't wait!!!! 😆😆😆😆

Daniel: I gotta go. Break is over. I love you, baby. 😊😊😊😊

Angelica: I love you too. I will see you soon, baby 😳😳😳😳😳

I was so excited that she was coming. I went back behind the counter to work with what must have been the biggest smile on my face. There were no new customers, so I stood there daydreaming like I was still in high school.

"Daniel," Torrie interrupted my thoughts, "Please check that the restrooms are clean."

"Absolutely," I said, still halfway in la-la land. As I walked toward the restrooms, I was sure I heard Torrie snort with laughter. That was fine, though. I was madly in love, and I know Torrie wouldn't ever really make fun of me. Okay, maybe a little, but she would swear she was laughing with me, not at me. When I finally walked back behind the counter, I wasn't sure If she actually checked the bathrooms or just assumed they were clean enough.

When Angelica walked in, I almost jumped over the counter. "Hi, baby," I said.

"Hi." She smiled. "This is my little brother, Noah." She gestured to the little boy with her. I figured he looked to be about seven years old.

"Hi, buddy," I said to him.

"Hi," he waved to me.

"Do you like to bowl?" I asked him.

"Uh-huh," he answered.

"That's great, because you get a free game today." I told him.

"Awesome!" He got excited.

I gave them their bowling shoes, then directed them to

their lane. I promised her I would have another break before she had to leave. It was mostly a slow day, so I stood behind the counter watching the two of them bowl. It was in that moment that a thought struck me. It was both a wonderful and terrifying thought. One day she just might be over their bowling with our son. Or daughter. Or both. Who knows what was to come for us. I smiled at the thought of us starting a family one day. One day after college, of course.

I was beyond happy when it was break time again. I went and sat at her table with a pitcher of coke and a few glasses. Angelica sat down with us. Her little brother came over to the table too. She poured him some coke. After he drank it, I called him over to me. I took out my wallet.

"Here, buddy," I said, handing him a five dollar bill, "Go get some quarters and play some arcade games."

"Awesome." He jumped up and down. "Thank you." He ran toward the games.

I looked at Angelica. "So, Friday night, dinner and the movies?" I asked, though I think it sounded more like a statement.

"That sounds amazing." She smiled. "Oh, and thank you for being so kind to Noah."

"You're welcome," I said. I felt that was the only necessary response.

We sat there talking until she said she had to leave.

FOUR YEARS LATER

I walked across the stage when my name was called. I was finally graduating from college, as was Angelica. I was now receiving my bachelor's degree in history. Afterward, I asked to speak for a minute. My request was granted and I was handed the mic.

"This has been an amazing four years," I said to the crowd. Looking around at the uncertain faces, I smiled and said, "Don't worry, I am not going to bore you with some long ridiculous speech that you won't remember ten minutes after you leave." That got some chuckles and applause. "I will just cut right to the chase."

"Angelica, if you would please join me on the stage," I said. She walked up and joined me. I took one of her hands in mine.

"Angelica, I love you, and I want to show you how much!" I said. I knelt to one knee and pulled out a ring. She put her hand over her mouth in awe. Tears were forming in her eyes.

"Angelica, will you marry me?" I proposed.

"Yes, yes I will," she accepted with tears streaming down her face. I put the ring on her finger, then we kissed.

When we pulled apart, I said, "Baby, I recall the day we met. You slipped and nearly took me down."

She laughed through her tears. "I love you so much, Daniel," she said.

"Angelica," I said to her, "I love you too, and I want you to know that even when you slip, I promise, I'll never let you fall."

You Make Me Wanna
La'Keah Shannelle

Summary

Two friends have a strange night where the things that happen force them to acknowledge their feelings. The snow blows all while their hidden longing for one another comes out.

Biography

LaKeah Shannelle is a new author from Cincinnati, Ohio. She discovered her love of the written word fairly early in life. Always with a book in hand, she decided why not touch the hearts of others as hers has been. A lover of people and the human emotion, she will keep you engrossed with every word, no matter what genre she takes on. Take the challenge and go on the adventure with her.

You Make Me Wanna
La'Keah Shannelle

Chapter 1

As LeAndria Adams sat on her couch, she continued to flip through the stations on her cable TV.

"Lelee, if you didn't find anything the first two times you went through all two hundred channels, then you're not gonna find anything this time," she murmured to herself as she put down the remote.

Feeling bored and anxious, she walked into the kitchen and got a carton of fudge ripple, a spoon, and then walked back into her living room. On the way there, she stopped to look at her favorite spot in her house. Above her couch was a big picture of her and her best friend, Keondre' at their high school graduation ten years ago. Someone had taken their picture right as they saw each other and embraced. Their eyes were full of tears as they held each other.

Just the thought of that moment and the way it made her feel brought on a new wave of tears. Shortly after that day, Keon went off to school in Virginia, while she stayed in their small Ohio town and attended the state college there. They wrote and called each other often. Every birthday, holiday, and special occasion, they sent each other cards, and every blue moonflowers. They never lost touch in the eight years he was gone.

She walked all the way into the room, then sat down. When she opened the carton of ice cream, she smiled as she saw the chocolate swirls in the container. They reminded her of Keon's smooth skin.

"Girl, you have got it bad," she laughed to herself. Truthfully, she did, and had since she was fifteen. His sweet chocolate looks combined with his gentlemanly ways made it hard not to love him. He was the total package with the brains included. He had attended medical school on a full scholarship he earned not just with his grades, but by winning a competition. Now, he was one of the only black obstetricians in their area. After a ton of education for herself, she now worked in the same hospital as he did. Her career choice was close to his. She was a nurse midwife while he was an actual doctor. They saw each other often.

Looking down, she realized \ she had eaten half the carton of ice cream. Getting up, she put it away in the freezer. Stripping off her top and bra on her way to the bathroom, she discarded her dirty clothes in the hamper and turned on the shower to let it warm up. Going up the hall to get her nightie, she stopped to inspect herself in the mirror. She felt like she was slightly overweight, but that was okay. Her bust line was a glorious size, her hips and bottom beautifully large and in charge. In retrospect, her size eighteen twenty body was sleek, well-toned, and tight. Her light brown eyes took in her looks and she smiled. Her dimples flashed back at her which made her laugh because she knew she was pretty. Remembering her shower, she raced to the bathroom before it got cold.

She had just begun to enjoy her pampering when she was pulled from her peaceful cocoon by a loud pounding that could not have been anything but her front door.

"Who the..." she never completed the thought as the pounding continued on.

"Wait," she yelled to her rude intruder. She quickly jumped out of the shower and threw on her lavender sarong style nightgown. She walked to the door still partially wet. When she got there, she threw open the door.

"Wha—" she never finished because she was shocked by what she saw.

Chapter 2

Keondre' Myles breathed a sigh of relief as he made it to LeAndria's door. He had barely made it to her apartment. He began to pound on her door to match the pounding in his head. Two minutes later, he heard her yelling at the door. What she said, he didn't understand. Too tired to care, he leaned against the door and waited for her to open it.

As the door whipped open, he realized a little too late that he shouldn't have leaned against it. The fall was so quick, he didn't have time to yell out, but he did moan softly as he landed on the softest surface he had ever felt in his life. He closed his eyes as he rubbed his face in the soft down and snuggled closer. He knew then and there that he was truly drunk because he could have sworn he was lying against a soft body. He smiled at the thought.

"Keon! Get your heavy butt off of me," Lelee yelled at him. Not that she really wanted him to. He felt like her biggest fantasy come true, but he was a big man. The feeling of his face against her brought on an electric storm that zinged through her whole body. Oh, Lord, she was getting ready to embarrass herself. She had to get up. "Keon, please. You are heavy. I can't breathe." It was true, but darn, it was nice. He never listened to her, and he would pick now to move and finally obey something she said.

"Lelee, is that you?" He slurred his words horribly, "I'm so glad I made it to the door. I went to Brett's bachelor party and I think that I had too much to drink." He said all this as he stumbled, trying to get off the floor. "I left and walked here. I barely made it. Thank goodness you live just around the corner of the bar."

"Keon, why would you drink? You know you can't handle anything with alcohol in it. The last time you drank was when you passed a big exam in college and you drank a couple of beers. You called me and said some crazy things, which even today, I still don't get. Alcohol always makes you act crazy. You always end up saying and doing things you want to take back when you're sober. That was the first and last time you drank to my knowledge. Why did you do it tonight?"

The whole time she was talking, he was just staring at her. He had always thought that she was pretty, but whether it was alcohol-induced or not, she looked beautiful. He now knew that the soft surface he rested on was her. He should have known. He had been memorizing everything about her since he was a teen. Even the sweet aroma that was her unique smell.

Right now, she was slightly wet, and that thing she was wearing should be outlawed.

"Sorry, Lelee." He realized that he had gotten her out of the shower. "Let me help you up so you can sit down."

He quickly helped her up. She was not that big, so it wasn't hard. While he walked to the couch, she turned around and closed the door, locking it.

"Lelee, I can't make it home like this. Can I stay here with you tonight? I can sleep on the couch. I won't get in the way, I promise."

Swallowing hard, it took her a moment to answer him.

"Sure, honey, you can stay as long as you like," she answered with a tight throat.

Chapter 3

After two pots of coffee, LeAndria hoped Keon's intoxication was wearing off, because for the last two hours, he had been sending her steamy looks that could melt steel. It was hard work trying to not notice his staring eyes. She felt her heart bubbling and humming just like the pot of coffee she was making. Even though she was sober, she felt like she had been enchanted with a strong drink as he had been.

"Are you feeling better?" she asked him quietly.

"Yeah, I do. Funny, but I only had one beer, and I can remember everything that happened tonight. It's weird. It's like my body is not my own."

"What do you mean?" she asked in concern.

"I can't quite explain it. I feel like I slowed down."

"Were you with Brett the whole night?"

"No, we all met at this bar by the hospital first, then we went to the place where he had his party."

"Did you drink anything while you were there?"

"Yeah, a coke."

"That's it? No alcohol?"

"That's it."

"Keon, is it possible you could have been drugged? I mean, you have been acting awfully strange." She smiled in a teasing manner. "And not the usual strange way you act when you've had too much to drink. You definitely seem a little off."

Fully blushing was something he didn't do often, but right now, he was beet red. He was hoping she didn't notice his hard stares. He could usually hide it just fine, but tonight, he was open to any and everything, and it was getting harder and harder to keep his mouth shut.

"You don't notice anything any other time. What made you see it today?"

"What did you say?" she asked from her place at the counter. She had only half heard him because she was busy making the coffee. She was wondering if there was an answer as to why he was behaving so strangely.

Getting up from his spot on the couch, he stalked over to her and leaned in. He wanted her to know the way she made him feel. He was tired of the games and the pretending. He had wanted her for too long. Had since he was young.

"I said that you don't notice any other time, so what made you notice it today?" he asked as he leaned into her and wrapped his arms around her waist.

When she leaned into him, she quickly came to her senses. Lelee turned around, which may have been a big mistake. Looking into his beautiful green/gold eyes, she deeply inhaled.

"I think you need to go and sit down. You are very unsteady on your feet and you're not thinking clearly."

"I'm thinking just fine and I don't want to sit down. I like where I am at this moment."

If it was possible, he seemed to move even closer to her. As he did, Lelee tried to move away from him. He anticipated this move and he trapped her in by putting his arms on either side of her body. He was so close that she smelled his cologne, saw his flushed skin, and even saw the small beads of sweat that ran down the side of his face.

"Keon, you're sweating. Are you hot?"

"Yeah, I am," he said through his clenched teeth. Then he smiled that deep dimpled sexy smile he had and added, "Did you know you have the sweetest eyes that I have ever seen, and did you know that you have a banging body?"

All of this information was delivered to her while he ran his hand up and down her side. The gentle glide of his hand was making her breath come out in shaky puffs.

"Keon, I really think you need to see a doctor. I truly think someone put something in your drink tonight."

"That's funny. Did you forget I am a doctor, and I think that I would know the signs of being drugged?"

"Keon, please let me help you sit down," she begged him in a sweet tone of voice. This was not easy, especially considering that he was in her face.

"Okay, but the only way I will let you help me is if you kiss me," he whispered close to her ear. The silkiness of his breath tickling her skin made her shiver. That small moment in time made her drop her guard, and move closer into his embrace.

"LeAndria, please," he sighed into her ear, and the side of her neck.

She was outdone by the sound of his voice, his breath on the sensitive skin on her neck, and by him gently saying her name. Raising her hands, she placed one on his firm chest, and the other one she placed on the side of his face. Slowly leaning into him, she closed her eyes and did what felt right. Placing her lips against his, she added just a small amount of pressure, just enough for her to feel the softness of his skin.

Well, it was her intention to just keep it simple, but he had something else on his mind entirely. As she went to move away from him, he grabbed the sides of her face and began an assault against her lips. Gently nibbling her mouth as if he was hungry and she was his only meal. He slowly licked the seam of her mouth to get access, and the slow and sexy feel of this had her body burning and humming badly. Not able to help herself any longer, she opened her mouth to his warmth and allowed him entry. From this moment on, she knew that neither of them would be able to walk away from this.

Chapter 4

When her mouth opened, he moaned what suspiciously sounded like thank you. The first brush of his lips against hers, and she almost went up in smoke, the second, she did.

He knew she would be like this; fire and smoke. He reached behind her and pulled her hair free from the clip it was held up in. Throwing the clip to the floor, he pushed his hands into her hair, and massaged her scalp. Never in his life had a simple kiss blown his mind to bits as this one had, and he knew no other ever would again.

Knowing this was going to go too fast too quickly, she knew she would have to be the one to stop. Plus, there was the small issue of whether he had been drugged or not.

Pulling back so he had no choice but to release her lips, she looked deep into his eyes.

"Okay, you got your kiss and then some. You promised that if you got a kiss, you would sit down." For a minute, she thought he was going to grab her again (not that she didn't want him to), but instead, he smiled a deep smile at her and walked to her couch.

Going to sit back on the couch with him, LeAndria grabbed his arm and took his pulse. With a sideways glance, she took his respiration rate, and both were high and erratic.

"Keon, let me look into your eyes," she spoke strongly, even though she didn't feel strong. Not waiting for his reply, she leaned in and looked into his pupils, which were dilated, and where he was hot and sweaty before, now seemed cold and clammy.

"Keon, are you cold?"

"Yeah, I am, but I know it's because you moved so far away from me."

"Maybe." Knowing she needed to get him checked out, she got up to grab the cordless phone.

"Hello, this is Dr. Brett Thomas' on-call service, may I

help you?" the voice on the phone stated.

"Yes, you can. This is LeAndria Adams and I'm calling on behalf of Dr. Keondre' Myles..."

After fighting with Keon and having to promise him more kisses (some she did give), she got dressed, then packed him up in her Bronco and drove him straight to the hospital, which was no easy task, having to struggle with a two hundred plus pound man with tentacles for arms. Thank the sweet Lord for the fact that Dr. Thomas got his message quickly, because he met them in the emergency room. Now she was sitting and waiting for someone to come and tell her what was going on with him.

"LeAndria." Upon hearing her name, she quickly jumped out of her seat to go over to talk to Dr. Thomas. He was a nice looking man with sexy blonde looks and golden eyes. He and Keondre' had met in medical school and had become good friends. Now, they were the best of friends and inseparable.

"How is he?" she said quietly.

"Well, he's fine now. He was drugged though; we found a small trace in his blood. Evidently, he didn't get the full dose. He must not have drunk his whole drink."

"What was it?"

"We have to wait for the tox screen before we can tell, but I'm suspecting it was a hint of ecstasy. We really can't do anything, but flush his system, and watch him closely."

"Can he go home?"

"Yes, but he needs someone to watch him overnight. Since you brought him here, can he stay with you and you keep an eye on him?"

"I wouldn't have it any other way." Pausing for a second, she got up the courage to ask her question. "Will he remember anything he said or did tonight?"

The way she asked the question made him raise an eyebrow for a second. Knowing how his friend felt about her (that secret revealed one night in college when he got drunk), he wondered what his friend had done tonight to make this beauty with the honey-colored skin blush.

"What did he do that he needs to forget?" he teased.

"I can't tell you that. I mean, that's between us, and if he doesn't remember, then it will be just between me and me alone. I'm sorry, I know you're his friend, but I am too, and I think that he wouldn't want this out. Can you understand that?"

"Yeah, I can, but, shoot, it would have been some good dirt," he said with a big smile.

With that settled, they both laughed at the absurdity of his comment.

While they laughed, he took her in the back to where Keon was. When she walked into the room, she had to hold her breath just to calm herself down. She knew he was gorgeous, but this was ridiculous. He lay on the bed without anything on but his jockey shorts and his socks, fast asleep. Walking over to him, she bent over and kissed him on the forehead.

"I'll take care of you tonight," she whispered.

When he heard her voice, he opened his eyes and she had to pause because of the look in his eyes—they spoke of something she refused to acknowledge.

Chapter 5

"Hello, Doc. I see you're awake. We're discharging you now. Here are a few instructions. Get plenty of rest, and drink plenty of fluids. You should not be alone for the next twenty-four hours."

The nurse then turned to her.

"I assume you'll be taking care of him. I know you got all the instructions, and here are a few papers on his condition. He just needs to sign these papers and we're done here," His nurse spoke while she disconnected his IV. After she was done, she handed them the papers. Helping him sign the discharge papers and get all of his final instructions, LeAndria began to gather his clothes for him.

When Keon sat up on the side of the bed, he realized how weak he was. He didn't think he could get up all on his own.

"Lelee, I think that I am going to need help. I'm sorry."

"What are you sorry for? I'm here for you. I'm just glad you are safe and that you didn't get a lot of that stuff."

"I got enough to make my vitals go crazy. I just thank God that I made it to your house. Thank you for taking care of me like you did and bringing me here. Things could have been a lot worse."

"You know you're my boy and if I could help it, nothing would ever happen to you."

Quickly looking away before she said or did something stupid like telling him she loved him or kissed him, she got his undershirt and began to help him with it.

Raising his arms above his head, he allowed her to help him into his shirt. But for the life of him, He couldn't take his eyes off of her face and the way her hair swept around her shoulders or the hot honey glow in her eyes. He could remember just about everything that had happened. Some things were a blur, but the main things he wouldn't forget.

She had wanted him just as much as he had wanted her.

Trying not to touch his chest as she pulled down his undershirt, she had to stop and let out a breath with the effort. It had been years since she had seen him without his shirt on and when she saw it last, it didn't look so wide, and it wasn't sprinkled with little fine hairs like it is now. Before he thought her strange, she reached out to pull it all the way down.

He saw her hands shake, so he reached out and grabbed them in his. He must have startled her because she looked up at him as if she forgot he was there. He no longer cared about her seeing his feelings, so he reached out his unsteady hand and trailed a finger down the side of her face.

"Come here." He spoke the words so softly, she almost thought she imagined them. Seeing the look in his eyes, she walked into his arms. Tenderly wrapping her in his arms, he pulled her up against him and held her like he had wanted to for years—pressed close to heart. He held her close with his face in her hair, the sweet smell of her, the essence of who she was. In that hug, he let her feel all of his feelings for her, so much that it brought a spot of moisture to his eyes because for the life of him, he felt she was indeed doing the same thing.

Chapter 6

Remembering where they were, he let her go, and jumped down from his spot. Seeing his body half clothed made her heart jump. She felt that she was the one who needed to see a doctor.

"Lelee, go get the car. I'll be out front by the time you return."

"Keon, I can't leave you to do this on your own. You said you needed help."

"I think that I can handle it now. Go. You need some space. Take it now because you may not get a chance to it later."

Looking at him, she didn't know exactly how he meant that. Agreeing with him that she did need some space, she walked out of the room and went to get the car.

Smiling to himself, he meant exactly what he said. He may never give her space again.

Running into her apartment as fast as they could to get out of the snow, they were both out of breath by the time they got inside. It had started snowing when they stopped at his place for a change of clothes. Rubbing her hands together quickly to get warm, she started to unpack the bags of groceries she had brought from the store.

"Are you hungry or thirsty?" she asked.

Not getting an answer, she turned to see if he was okay, and saw him standing by the couch, looking at the picture of them together.

"Look how young we were. Did you see our lives going like it has? What did you want at that age?"

"I don't remember what I wanted at that age. Heck, sometimes I don't think I know what I want now." She shook her head as she replied.

He looked at her for a moment while he ran his hands over his close-cropped face, then ran his hands over his perfectly groomed goatee and beard. Tired of skirting around his feelings, he turned his green/gold eyes on her.

"Are you sure about that, because sometimes I think you know exactly what you want, but you're too scared to go after it. What I don't get is why you're so scared." He looked her deep in her eyes and smiled.

"Okay, I refuse to touch that one with a ten-foot pole. I'm gonna go and put the groceries away and then I'm gonna go and take a shower and put on some clean clothes."

Before she could turn all the way around and walk away, he caught her by the arm.

"Aren't you tired of running yet? It's going to come to a point where you can't run anymore. And when you stop, Lelee, I'll be there."

Just the intense look in his eyes made her stop in her tracks. When he reached out and touched her cheek, she leaned into his touch.

"You know, sometimes you make me wanna…" At the look on her face, he knew it was too much for her to take, so he stopped.

"Just go ahead and take your shower. I'll put the groceries away, and don't worry about making the bed in the other room. I'll get it."

"Why don't you finish what you have to say?"

"Go before I change my mind."

With that, she turned and went for her shower.

"You can't run forever," he whispered.

Chapter 7

Lying in the bed, staring at the ceiling, Keon couldn't get the vision of Lelee out of his mind. He had first met her when his family moved to their town when he was fifteen. Tired of moving, he had a very bad attitude when they arrived. No matter how much his mom and dad told him this would be the last time, he just felt like they weren't telling him the truth.

Sitting on the front porch sulking and looking for impending doom to fall down, he was startled when he heard the most melodious voice he had ever heard in his young life.

"Hello, my name is LeAndria Adams, and I live next door. I just wanted to introduce myself and say welcome."

The simplest words, but they changed and impacted his life in a mighty way. In his mind, he fell in love that day, but over the years, he knew it was just puppy love, a cute and sweet crush. When he went away to college, he didn't think about her in that context until he heard her voice on the phone or until he went home for a visit, then his heart would flutter a thousand miles a minute.

Just thinking about her honey gold looks made his heart jump. Her hair long and thick hung past her shoulders, her eyes a golden brown, her skin more honey that rippled over fine bones and a thick full physique. They often ran together so he knew she was in great shape. Oh, and her legs were long. She almost always came close to beating him. Still hot and groggy from the drug, he kicked off the thin sheet he had on. Sitting up in the bed, he went to look out at the night. It was still snowing, and now ice was all in the mix. Walking into the dark kitchen, he poured himself a cup of juice. After rinsing out his cup, he slowly walked back to his room. When he passed her door, he stopped. He hadn't realized before that the door was slightly open. Not being able to resist, he peeked inside. Lying in the bed on her stomach with one leg slightly bent, LeAndria had kicked off her covers and was silhouetted by the street lights outside. Before he knew it, he was walking into her room and standing next to her bed. Kneeling down next to her bed, he lightly ran his hands over her glorious mane, and bent to kiss her exposed shoulder. Sitting back, he sat and looked at her beauty, and as if she felt his presence, she cracked open her eyes just a bit. Then she did something that shocked him. She rolled over and reached out her hand for him to join her.

Opening her eyes to her dream man, she smiled at the fact that he finally had come to her side. Touching the face that she had wanted for so long, she blinked back a wave of tears that threatened to overflow.

Seeing her tears, and understanding them, he leaned in and kissed the hurt away, realizing for the final time he truly loved this woman and that he would never let her go.

"You make me wanna love you fully, thoroughly, unconditionally, any way you want me to. Just as long as you let me love you."

Epilogue

LeAndria faced the picture of her and Keon on their graduation day and smiled. One day they would have one heck of a story to tell their children and great grands. A story of two scared teens who grew into adults that harbored the same irrational fear.

Too scared to tell the other how much they cared for each other and scared to say how much they wanted to love each other openly.

LeAndria rubbed her emerging belly and smiled at the twinkling diamond on her finger. The tree in the corner sparkled just as bright. The snow was a perfect blanket laid upon the Earth for all to cherish. It was such a pretty night.

"Little one, Daddy will be home soon to take care of us. I know you are ready. So am I."

LeAndria was grateful for her blessings and the ones that were soon to come.

George's Christmas Eve
Sonya McKinzie

Summary

Eve and George were partners at one of the largest technology firms and had worked together for several years before they really took the time to get to know one another. After building a strong friendship, they confided in one another often, but they didn't expect their friend would go from casual to intimate to committed. Both had lost their companions under uncontrollable circumstances, broken and unsure of their future. They chose to spend the Christmas holiday together, and on Christmas Eve, they realized they were in love and destined to be more than friends. This chapter takes you on a walk through grieving a lost one to embracing new love and life after the loss of a companion.

Biography

Born and raised in Brunswick, Georgia, Sonya McKinzie is the executive director and founder of Women of Virtue Transitional Foundation Inc. (WOVTF), which was established in February 2016. She is a single mommy to an amazing eight-year-old daughter, McKinzie Alise, who she considers to be her greatest gift from God. A sixteen-year, second-generation survivor of domestic violence, she worked hard to obtain numerous degrees: MA and BA degrees in human services counseling, business administration, and is pursuing her second masters in public relations. Sonya has victim advocacy, human resources specialist, leadership, and management specialist certificates, as well as is a five-time bestselling author and avid blogger. Sonya is passionate about working to empower, encourage, and uplift girls and women to be more and love more without faltering. Sonya uses her testimony as a connection to her readers.

Contact Info:

Email: womenofvirtuefoundation@gmail.com

Website: http://www.perfectly-imperfect-womenofvirtue.com/

Blog: https://darkskinisbeautiful.wordpress.com/

George's Christmas Eve
Sonya McKinzie

We were married, but not to each other.

George put the key into the slot and when the door unlocked, he stepped back to allow me to enter the room first. We were both silent, and perhaps a little uneasy about our situation. The hotel room was exquisite, the high, vaulted ceilings were asymmetrical and adorned with crystal chandeliers. There was a plush, white sofa with a fireplace in the sitting area with a fruit tray and champagne on the center table, greeting us when we entered. To the left, I could see the beautiful king-sized bed, candles were set up on either side of the bed, and there was a fluffy pillow on the chaise at the end of the bed. The fragrance of honey and roasted almonds lingered in the air – it was like a story from one of those romance novels. The bed was covered with a purple and lilac colored bedspread. Lilac curtains and purple sheers framed the tall windows; the thin frames led the way in the moonlight. The carpet was thick, lush and tan-colored. Christmas décor was strategically placed around the room, a beautifully handcrafted ornament was at the bedside near the hotel's in-house restaurant menu. The fragrance of candy-canes and honey-roasted pecans lingered in the air – it was like a story from one of those romance novels.

Looking over my shoulder, I could see George taking in the ambiance just as I was – then he slowly moved past me to put our luggage down. Shortly thereafter, he touched my shoulder and asked, "Eve, are you okay?"

"Oh, yes – sure. I am just enjoying how beautiful this suite is. The company really splurged on our hotel suites this year, I cannot believe that we are here in Savannah"

For the past two years, George and I spent our Christmas holidays at the annual IT trade shows representing Gee-Pele Software Inc. – introducing our forthcoming products due to release the following year. This year, George and I were both nervous because we would be introducing one of the largest product releases of the twenty-year history of the company. Because this was our twentieth-year anniversary, our CEO wanted to make a huge statement and she felt that George and I would best represent the company.

"Eve, we have the world on our shoulders! But I am confident knowing you are here with me. I could not begin to imagine when Gee-Pele would do without you as the vice president in the IT Department," George shared.

"You have such confidence in me – I wish I had just a portion of it. Oddly enough, I don't feel that I am as prepared as I should be with all the last-minute work I had to put in before our flight left this morning. *That* means we will be spending some time together this evening going over the content and blueprints for the 2019 product line. If you don't disagree, why don't we relax a bit and then get together later for a bite to eat this evening? Does that sound good to you?" I asked.

"I have no arguments about that – I am in room number 1254. Call me if you need anything. In the meantime, let's plan to meet around eight in the dining room downstairs. I will be waiting with Christmas bells on," George joked.

Sitting on the chaise, I looked at my beautiful wedding ring and remembered the day that I became Mrs. Eve Walker. I was so young and full of love. Then my eyes began to tear up as I remembered my late husband, Christopher Walker, and how he had been taken away from me too soon. The only good memory that reassured me was that he died in the line of duty while in Afghanistan and doing what he loved to do, fighting for our country.

Thinking back over the hard times, years of grieving, and feeling that I would never be able to rebuild my life, nor live without him, I was grateful I had faith in God. Because when they told me he was gone, I wanted to die too.

As a lieutenant, Christopher had spent more than nine years in the army and was so proud of his highly decorated lapels on his uniform. So was I. But the day the officers appeared at my front door was the most devastating day of my life. It was three days after Christmas. I remember them telling me, "I am sorry for your loss, Mrs. Walker, Lieutenant Walker was one of the best officers we have ever known."

It felt like I was caught in a dead zone. I couldn't breathe, and I fell straight to my knees and passed out for what seemed like forever. Thankful that Maya, my older sister was with me to help brace the fall, she was able to guide me so that I didn't hurt myself.

The days, weeks, months, and years to follow were indescribable. All my feelings of anger resulted in peaks and valleys where I would scream, cry, and sit in silence. Those feelings and actions that I expressed all at once were tremendous – I had lost everything. At least, he was my everything! We didn't have an opportunity to start a family – we were married for eight years and both felt we should wait a while before we started a family, especially since he had been away for most of our marriage. Fresh out of high school, we both made choices that seemed were right at the time. We wanted our family to have a stable lifestyle and didn't want to struggle if there was a need for me to stay home with our children.

I remember Christopher telling me, "Don't worry, baby, I will serve ten years and then we will be all set to purchase a home. Loans will be paid off and we can enjoy our lives together."

That was eight years prior to his death, and when we decided to wait a little longer, especially since he had progressed in his profession so quickly, and I in mine.

I never thought I would be a widow at the age of twenty-seven. Not everyone is blessed to meet and spend their lives with a soul mate. I was convinced that I would never be able to love again. To be fair, I couldn't say that I even took the time to grieve Christopher's death. Instead, I threw myself into my job at Gee-Pele Software Inc., starting out from the grown floor as a programmer in the IT department and quickly working my way up to the vice president's role over the information systems and technology department within two years of my hire date. I was the only black woman to become a vice president at Gee-Pele Software Inc., and the youngest. Last year, I received the ATFLA Leadership Award from the American Technology in the Florida Leadership Association and was being considered for a promotion to the COO position within the next six months. With all the achievements and blessings – none of it compared to the reward I had in being

Christopher's wife.

Knock. Knock.

"Yes?" I responded.

"Eve, it is after eight forty-five. Are we still meeting for dinner to go over the blueprints?" George asked.

"Yes, of course. Why don't we plan to order room service and work in the office space in my room? I apologize, I laid down for a moment and really lost track of time," I responded.

"Sure, that is fine. Besides, the restaurant downstairs closes in about ten minutes," George said.

George and I spent the next several hours perfecting the PowerPoint presentation, notes, and finalizing the product presentations in preparation for a long grueling meeting. The night ended around midnight and I was exhausted. George was too.

"George, I think I am going to drive to Savannah for the weekend. I need a restful and relaxing weekend, so you will be taking a flight back alone," I joked.

"Wow that sounds fun. How do you feel about having some company? I have a few family members there in the area and would love to go with you. I mean, if that is okay?" George inquired.

"Sure, only if you promise not to talk about work on the way there and do half of the drive," I replied. In my mind, I knew that while there was a need for some R&R, I certainly did not need to have it alone, as my mind was looping about Christopher, our lost plans, and how much I was missing him. It was hard to believe that my professional life was blossoming and growing very fast while my personal life was at a dark standstill. While thankful for the blessings for a career, I wanted Christopher and a family more.

As we drove through downtown Savannah, we made way to the Suffolk, a beautiful Savannah Bed and Breakfast – from the pictures, it looked to be the perfect location for a week of quiet and relaxation. George decided that he would also stay at the location. This would allow us an opportunity to hang out and a chance for him to show me around his hometown. I think we both were due to a bit of peace. George had been single for nine years and he seemed to be comfortable with his status. While I didn't know the extent of the demise of his relationship, what I did know, is over the past three years (before Christopher's death), we were great working partners, and as of recent, friends. He was a good person and he came from a great family upbringing and was a hard worker.

Upon our arrivals, we parted ways and checked into our rooms. All I could think about was a warm bath, washing my hair and enjoying the beauty of Savannah, Georgia. My room was warm and cozy. The room was adorned with southern and antique décor, and topped off with a beautiful fireplace and I could see a beautiful pond from the balcony connected to my room. The Portuguese-fashioned King-sized bed was breathtaking. I could not have made a better choice – I hoped George felt the same.

The bathroom was just as beautiful as the room itself. It was stocked with bath washes, oils, bombs, candles, chilled Moscato, and plush white towels. Starting a bath, I slipped on the bathrobe that hung on the Chinese shade. I wanted to scream inside, "Yessss." I have finally made it to a place of peace and relaxation. My body melted into the oversized bathtub, and the fragrance of lavender lingered in the air.

After taking a bath and throwing on shorts and a tee, there was a knock at my door.

"Yes?" I answered.

"Eve, it is George," he responded.

Opening the door, I looked to see a very relaxed George with a beautiful little girl who appeared to be six or seven years old with hazel brown eyes. She was like a china doll.

"Hi, Eve, I would like to introduce you to this sweet little princess. This is my niece, Amelia."

She was a small and beautiful six-year-old with curly black hair, and those eyes could melt the sun with their brightness. She had a hairband with little bunny ears on top. She seemed to be antsy and excited about hanging out with her uncle George and me for the day. As we exited the B&B, Amelia skipped from side to side as she held George's hand. Her personality was free and light-hearted, and she left me in awe. Immediately, I began to wonder what Christopher and my child would have been like. Would she/he have been a free-spirit like George or a busy-bee like me?

I took a deep breath as I enjoyed the lingering smell of River Sweet Treats in the air, combined with Amelia's happy-go-lucky presence. "Yummy, I smell pralines. I want some, please take me to it," Eve said.

"Don't you want to grab a bite to eat first? Remember, we haven't eaten today, and starting the day out with candy is not a good idea," George said.

"Awwww, Uncle George, please can we go? I promise I will only take one itsy bitsy bite and will eat all of my lunch. Pleaaaaseeee?" Amelia pleaded.

"Really, are you both ganging up on me? Alright, ladies."

As George pointed out a landmark near the entrance way of the B&B, we made our way to the car and told me some historical facts about the monument. He shared that he grew up in Savannah for the later part of his teenage years and how much he loved spending time there. Then they made their way to River Street Sweets.

We spent the entire day strolling down the streets, taking in the historical sites, and even took a ride on a riverboat. I think Amelia enjoyed it the most.

While I had worked with George for a long time, I didn't realize how much of a gentleman he was. Each building we entered, he was sure to hold the door open for us to enter and he would follow. At lunch, and while we had ice cream cones, he pulled our chairs out for us and made sure we had all our condiments before he sat down. He was a protector and old-fashioned Georgia man.

Later that evening, we parted and went our separate ways, but George shared that he wanted to drive out to Tybee Island the following morning, and advised me to wear a cool pair of shorts with comfortable shoes. I was excited to be getting away from the hustle and bustle of work, but most importantly, having someone cater to my needs. I had not had that since Christopher, and it felt odd, yet good, to be taken care of.

Sunday morning, I woke to a knock on my door and room service with a Caramel Macchiato, croissants, hazelnut butter with a side order of eggs. As I attempted to tip the service worker, he responded with a smile, "No, ma'am, please don't. This has been taken care of. Enjoy your day."

He exited my room.

How did George know what I liked to eat for breakfast? Had he been that observant over the past years we had worked together? Either way, this order hit the spot, and I was ready to start the day.

Around noon, George and I met in the lobby area. I was wearing a yellow sundress with sandals, and my hair was pulled up in a ponytail.

"Wow, you clean up nicely," George joked.

With George in his walking shorts, polo and sandals, he looked so handsome – it was a major difference between his stuffy suit. I was also shocked at how hot and humid it was in Savannah December twenty-first. I found it so odd, but I was not complaining about the seventy-five-degree weather.

"What are our plans for the day?" I asked.

"We are going to ride to Tybee Island, which is not too far away from our B&B." George smiled.

When we made it to George's convertible, he opened the car door for me. As I eased into the car, he placed his hand on the small of my back – it felt so strong and reminded me of the last time I had been touched by a man, who my deceased husband, Christopher. In my mind, I was beginning to wonder what was happening, but whatever was happening, I didn't want it to stop.

As I watched him walk around the car and get in, he asked, "Are you ready?"

I responded, "Hell, yes – let's do it."

As we rode down the highway toward Tybee Island, we began to smell seafood, and it was delightful.

"Oh, my goodness, I am such a foodie, George. Can we stop and see where that delicious smell is coming from?" I asked.

George began to laugh and said, "Of course we can. As a matter of fact, we cannot leave without having some good old southern crab boil."

Stopping at The Crab Shack on Estill Hammock Road, George stopped the car and walked around to my door and opened it. He held his hand out to assist me with gracefully getting out of his very low corvette.

Again, he placed his hand on the small of my back and guided me into the restaurant.

I kept thinking this man was so gentle, attentive, and caring – he seemed like someone I could befriend, that I could consider a best friend.

Once our server took our orders, George said, "Is this okay?" He leaned in toward me to make sure I could hear his voice over the loud activity going on around us.

"Yes, this is perfect," I responded.

The restaurant was playing jazz music, and everyone seemed to be having a great time. At least I knew I was. When we were done with our meal, George and I debated about who would pay for the meal. George won the debate.

"Thank you, that food was so amazing!" I smiled.

"You are more than welcome. Now, let's go to the beach. I would like you to see the Southside. It is so peaceful there," George said.

"That sounds great," I responded.

As the wind whipped through my hair and against my face, I looked over at George. He was looking at me, and the look was like one I had never seen – at least not from him.

"What? Why are you looking at me like that?" I asked.

"Because you look different. You are beautiful. More beautiful when you are relaxed," George said, looking away.

Reaching over to touch his face gently, I said, "Thank you, I appreciate you and all you have been doing for me this weekend."

His face followed the touch of my hand, and then he reached up to grab my hand. He pulled my hand over to his lap and held it. Then he lifted my hand up to his lips and kissed it.

I could not bear to look in his eyes because I was confused about what was happening and what I was feeling inside. Was I wrong for allowing myself to be open to the possibilities of loving another man after losing Christopher?

"Are you Okay?" he asked.

"Yes," I responded.

The remainder of the thirty-two-minute drive was awkward, quiet, and different. The silence between us stretched from seconds to minutes, and the silence became slightly unbearable. I felt that we needed to say something, but neither of us knew what. All the while, he was holding my hand tightly.

George cleared his throat. "Eve, I hope you are Okay with me holding your hand," George inquired.

"Yes, I am fine with it," I said in an uncertain tone.

"May I share the story behind my nine years of being single?" George asked.

"Of course – please do," I responded.

"When I was in college, I dated a young lady who was my first love – my first everything. Her name was Lillie and we dated for about a year when we found out she had cancer. She died about six months after her diagnosis. The cancer was found too late for chemo and any treatment. Lillie was amazing, and I felt that she would be my wife – she completed me. In this instance, I decided to focus on myself solely from a professional standpoint and try to deal with the grief of losing her. I decided I would be abstinent until I was ready to give my heart again. And here I am, nine years later – still single – and in love with you," George said.

His words "and in love with you" took my breath away – I couldn't understand why me. When and how did he develop these feelings about me?

Sitting in silence, I didn't know what to say.

George went silent and his hand slowly slipped away from mine. It was as if my silence embarrassed him and he somehow felt that he had overstepped boundaries.

"George, I – I mean, I really do care for you, too; but I am not sure I am in love," I responded. Inside my mind, I felt the same. I loved him, but as a friend, or maybe I wanted him to be my lover, I was confused."

George looked numb for a few minutes – then he said, "Well, sometimes you have to lose in order to win," which was the title of one of Fantasia Barrino's music tracks. He laughed nervously, and that was a clear indication that the remainder of our trip would either be awkward or enlightening.

Turning on to the oceanfront, which was the Southside of the beach,

George parked and said, "Let's do this!" He jumped out of the car and opened my door. He grabbed a black windbreaker, two beach towels, chips, wine coolers, and a small bucket from the trunk of his car.

He guided me toward an uncongested area of the beach and put our blankets down – then we set up our snacks.

"What's the bucket for, buddy?" I asked, laughing.

"Didn't you know – we are going to look for seashells and jellyfish." George smiled.

"Uhrrr, I am sorry you lost me at Jellyfish." I giggled.

We ran down to the beach, bare-footed, and wet our toes at the edge of the shore. It felt amazing and carefree.

George turned to me and said, "Are you happy, Eve?"

I answered, "George, I really am. This is a vacation that we both needed."

Stroking my hair in his hands and running his hands down the small of my back, he looked me in my eyes and said, "I know you are still grieving over Christopher, but I cannot lie to you. Eve, I really do love you. You are such a caring person and you deserve to be loved again. You deserve to have the family, picket fence, husband and children," George said with a serious look on his face.

Again, I was speechless – my heart was racing out of control.

George continued, "I know this is a lot to process, but I have been feeling this way for the past year, and with all of the work time we have spent together, I have had the time to get to know you both personally and professionally. This might seem crazy, or perhaps it makes sense, but Eve, I really do love you."

Looking in George's eyes, I could not lie nor deny my feelings – somehow, I felt that I cared for him too.

"George, I do care for you, but I feel that I am wrong. Is it too soon to love again?" I asked.

George looked at me and then he rubbed his hand up the small of my back again. It seemed to comfort me – then he said, "I cannot speak for Christopher, but I will speak for Lillie. She would want me to be happy. Because I believe I am destined to spend my life with the woman of my love. While I lost Lillie, I am still living, and I want a mate to complete me."

Leaning in, I kissed George lightly on his lips, and his embrace was strong and intense. I could feel my whole soul melting in his arms. It had been so long since another man had touched me, loved me, and made me feel that I was protected.

"George, I love you too. When I am with you, I feel like I am with my best friend, co-worker, and someone I can confide in and know I am not going to be judged," I said.

"I am so in love with you, Eve, and while it's exciting to know some of the feelings are reciprocated, I am also nervous because I don't want to lose what we already have – a beautiful friendship," George whispered.

"You know, perhaps it's because we have so much in common – more specifically the loss of a loved one, our mates. George, I am scared to lose our friendship too, but, I am even more afraid of not allowing these feelings to play out. I don't want to miss our chance to love again – but I don't want to make the wrong decision." I cried.

"It is getting chilly out. Why don't we go back to the bed and breakfast and have a snack, "George suggested.

"That sounds like a good idea," I said.

Before walking back toward our beach towel, George held me tighter and kissed my forehead, working his way down to my lips and kissed me strong. His touch sent chills down my spine and I melted like chocolate in his arms.

Returning to Savannah, we grabbed some ice cream from Dairy Queen and sat on the balcony and ate in our bedroom at the B&B.

"I cannot believe we are sitting here on Christmas Eve, eating ice cream and watching the water hitting the shore. This view is something like a scene from a magazine," I said, relieved and relaxed.

After finishing our ice cream, George took my hand and led me to the bathroom, ran me a bubble bath, and then told me to enjoy myself before closing the door. "I will be back in about thirty minutes," he yelled through the bathroom door.

Sitting back in the bathtub, I was thinking, well – this was a great day – at least we didn't have the pressure of the next step, and a part of me wanted him to take me, because we had teased each other for most of the evening with kisses and embraces. Perhaps we both needed to stop at that.

As I exited the bathtub, I heard a knock on the door – and I responded, "Yes?"

"It's me, Eve." The bathroom door opened and George was standing there.

Standing in my birthday suit, he walked over and covered me with a towel and walked me to the bedroom.

There were purple candles, wine, and chocolate covered figs at the bedside. Speechless, I followed him and allowed him to take me away.

Before I had time to say a word, George covered my lips with his. There was no persuading because I gave myself to him willingly. You could say we were like lovebirds, and we were on the same level. The warmth of his lips and arms around me felt like fireworks inside my body. The butterflies were taking over my stomach and I wanted to give myself to him wholly. As we deepened the kiss, our hearts opened, and we were two butterflies caught up in the net of love. After what seemed like forever, we separated, and I took his hand and walked him toward the bed – that was my way of saying, "Yes, I want you to take me."

My feelings were lustful and loving, and they were growing as the seconds passed us by.

George stood before me, beautiful, gentle, kind, and loving – it was like the feelings developed in a short period of time. Were the feelings always present, but they were suppressed? Why did it matter, because these thoughts were taking me away from the moment?

"Eve, may I make love to you?" George asked.

I responded, "There was no need to ask, George. I want this just as much as you do. Tonight, I give myself to you on Christmas Eve – this is my gift from me to you," I whispered.

After a night filled with passion and pillow talk – we knew we could not go backward. We were in love, connected, and committed to one another.

The following morning, I woke to George setting breakfast and pouring juice. "Wake up, sleepyhead – breakfast is ready." George smiled.

Grabbing my bathrobe, I walked over to the bathroom and brushed my teeth and washed up. Upon returning, George was standing with my chair pulled away from the table for me to sit down.

"Thank you," I said, and then reached over and kissed his hand gently.

After serving me my breakfast, George walked over to my side of the table and then went down on one knee and said, "Merry Christmas, Eve. Will you do me the honors of marrying me?" George asked.

I was speechless – "Oh my, George, are you serious? Please do not tease me. Are you sure you want to do this?" I asked in a high pitch tone.

"Yes, Eve. I could not be any surer than I am at this time – you are my destiny. Please let me love and take care of you. In my heart of hearts, I know that Lillie and Christopher would condone this. We are not supposed to be alone for the rest of our lives – this love that we share is rare. Our relationship as friends is solid. Our connection and commitment are stronger than ever before and last night solidified this. This is not lust in the heart. This is love, and I want to spend the rest of my life with you." George said, rubbing my face and kissing my forehead.

I was speechless. I could not believe that in one single weekend of silence, relaxation, and much communication, we were talking marriage.

"When did you get this beautiful ring?" I asked.

"I knew I wanted to ask you to marry me three months ago – I just didn't know when I would ask or if you would even have me as your husband, but I took a chance. I listened to you – one day you told me that your birthstone was opal, and so, I thought why not add that to this ring and make it extra unique and special like you, Eve," George responded.

"George, do you mind giving me a little time to think about this? Things are happening so fast," I responded.

"Oh, sure, yes. I understand," George said flabbergasted by my response. "I am going to make a few calls and wish everyone Merry Christmas – and find out what time dinner will be at my cousin's this evening," George said, exiting the room.

For several hours, I sat in the room thinking and rethinking the situation, wondering if I had made a mistake by saying I needed more time to decide when I already knew I wanted to be with George. Did I break his confidence?

What was I thinking?

I love this man – and here I am holding on to Christopher as if he can return to me. Some people never experience true love once in a lifetime, and here, God has presented me with another chance at love and a family. I'm turning it away.

About two hours later, George called and asked if I was ready to go out. "Sure, I will meet you in the lobby in about ten minutes," I said.

Walking into the lobby, I could see George standing by the fireplace in the main room,. He looked so handsome in his gray sweater and jeans. He was talking on his Bluetooth, so I stood from afar and watched him. He was beautiful from the inside out and I loved him. There was no second guessing – I knew he would take care of me and we would have a wonderful family – but I was afraid for some reason.

George noticed me standing across the room and he waved me to come to the fireplace as he wrapped up his call.

"George, I want to tell you something…I do love you. Please ask me again," I pleaded.

Looking at me, he kneeled down on one knee and pulled the ring from his pocket and said "Eve, will you marry me?" George asked with brightness in his eyes.

"George, yes, I will absolutely marry you. I love you," I responded.

For once in my life, I "jumped," and did the unexpected. I didn't overthink it. I just did it and allowed my heart to lead the way.

Standing there, we noticed several people were clapping and congratulating us and we sealed the agreement with a kiss.

"Thank you, God, for answering my prayers." George said.

Also available by

Anthologies

Sweet Candy Delights: Flash Fiction Stories
Holiday Chords: A Contemporary Romance Anthology
Worlds Apart: a Sci-fi Anthology

Coming in 2019

Etched in Stone: Rules to Abide By (A Ten Commandment Anthology)
Romantic Interludes: A Paranormal Romance
Mischief and Clovers: A St. Paddy's Day Flash Fiction Anthology
Eclipse: A Post-Apocalyptic World

Solo Novels

Sue Harmeling

Fishing with Reece (TBA)

Angela Kay

I Can Kill
The Naked Eye

Made in the USA
Columbia, SC
27 February 2019